Death Of A Ps

A Psychic Café M

(Book 8)

By

April Fernsby

www.aprilfernsby.com

Copyright 2020 by April Fernsby

Front Cover by www.coverkicks.com[1]

---

1. http://www.coverkicks.com

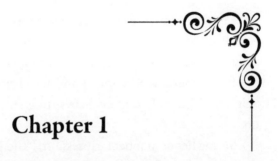

Chapter 1

I shivered as I looked around the café. "I don't understand why this is going ahead," I said to Peggy. "It's not the sort of thing we should be having here."

Peggy, my friend and neighbour, replied, "I'm surprised you feel like that considering your gift. I thought you'd be pleased to have another psychic here."

"I am, but not like this. Something's not right about it." I folded my arms.

"You mean because she's charging for readings and the like? Well, we've all got to make a living. If you've got a gift, then there's nothing wrong with making money out of it."

"I know. I'm not saying that, but it's the actual event which is bothering me. Who organised it? It wasn't me."

Peggy frowned. "I know. You've already told me that three times. And I've told you four times that it wasn't me either. Which only leaves your sister and her husband. They must have organised this spiritual evening, or whatever she's calling it. What's the psychic's name again? Teresa? Tracy?"

"It's Theodosia."

Peggy tutted. "What sort of a name is that?"

"A psychic kind of name?" I suggested. "Erin said she wasn't the one who booked the event. And Robbie's adamant that he didn't either."

"Pah! I wouldn't listen to a word those two say. You know how sleep-deprived they are."

I nodded. My sister Erin had given birth to twins two months ago. And little Maggie and Charlie seemed to think sleep was an optional activity and one which they didn't like much.

Peggy continued, "I don't know why Erin and Robbie won't let me help out. I keep offering my babysitting services, but they keep saying no."

Seeing her despondent expression, I said gently, "You've done more than enough to help them out. You know how stubborn Erin can be. She wants to do everything herself now, even if that means she's walking around like a zombie for the next few months until the twins sleep longer. She appreciated your help, you know that. You must do because she keeps telling you. But she can't rely on you forever."

"She can. I don't mind. I like to feel useful."

I put my hand on her arm. "I know you do. But you're still getting to see the twins nearly every evening. And it's after they've been fed and washed, so you get the best part of them."

Peggy brightened up. "I do. I love how they smell after their baths, and how cute they look in their little sleeping outfits. I know they can't understand a word I'm saying when I read those bedtime stories to them, but I love that special time I have with them."

"There you are, then. And you get weekends with them too. You're a major part of their lives. Little Maggie's face lights up when she sees you."

Peggy chuckled. "She's a bonnie baby. So is Charlie. I know you're right about Erin and Robbie wanting to be more responsible for their children. I do know that, but if it were up to me, I would have moved into their house and stayed there until the twins turned eighteen."

I laughed at that. "I know you would. But Erin's loss is my gain. I get your help this evening with this mysterious psychic event that no one seems to have organised." My eyes narrowed. "My money is on Erin. She's still working on the café website and checking online enquiries even though I told her not to. She probably said yes to Theodosia and then promptly forgot."

"Probably." Peggy gave me a long look. "Can't you use your psychic powers to find out who booked it?"

"I've told you before that I can't control them."

"You could try," Peggy insisted. "Why don't you get the website up on your phone, put your hand over the booking page, and see what happens. You might get one of those visions of yours."

I gave her a small smile. "I've already tried. Nothing happened."

"You haven't had a vision of any sort for a while now. Do you think you've lost your powers? Perhaps they've been transferred to Maggie or Charlie."

I shrugged. "I don't know if psychic abilities can be transferred. I think it's something you're born with. I'm glad I haven't had a vision because they're usually related to a murder."

Peggy nodded. "That's true. There's only one thing we can do to solve the mystery of this event and who organised it." Her glance went to the ceiling. "One of us should go upstairs and talk to whatshername. Ask her who booked this event."

I looked at the ceiling too. "You go. I've got things to do down here. And people will be arriving for the event soon. I'll need to open the door for them."

"I'm not going! You know what I'm like with stairs. And my hips are playing up. I'm a fragile old lady."

I snorted. "You're nothing of the sort! You are one of the healthiest people I know. I've seen you take those stairs two at a time sometimes. And since when did your hips start playing up?"

Peggy avoided my accusing gaze. "I don't want to go up there. I don't know why, but I've just got a weird feeling about the psychic upstairs."

"Me too. We didn't even hear her coming in. She must have sneaked in when we were in the kitchen. I only know she's up there because of that text she sent me. I meant to go up straight away to say hello, but..." I trailed off.

"But you don't want to see her either. A right pair of yellow-bellied cowards we are." Still avoiding my gaze, Peggy picked up a bit of fluff from her cardigan. "I think you should be the one to go up there. Talk to her as one psychic to another."

I was about to argue but then a knock at the café door stopped me. I cried out, "I'll get it!"

"No! I will!"

We both raced towards the door. Peggy ran at a super impressive speed.

I suddenly stopped. What was I doing? Would I rather race a pensioner across the café floor than say hello to a fellow psychic?

The answer was yes. I so did *not* want to meet Theodosia. I couldn't explain why, but I knew something awful was going to happen if we met.

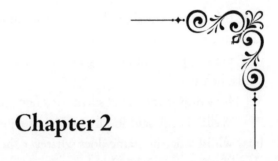

Chapter 2

I watched from the other side of the café as Peggy welcomed the customers in. Some of them looked excited, some appeared nervous, and others looked bewildered.

Peggy pointed to the stairs and explained where the psychic event was being held. I noticed she didn't lead them up the steps as she normally would for an event. She left them to go up on their own. I didn't blame her.

When the last person had ascended, Peggy came over to me and said, "I wonder how much they're paying for an appointment with her upstairs? I did ask a few people, but they were very evasive and I didn't get an answer. How much would you charge if you were doing this sort of a gig?"

"I wouldn't do this sort of gig."

"You should charge every time you help the police with their murder cases. If it weren't for you, most of their cases would remain unsolved. And I should charge for my services too. I have provided invaluable help to your detective boyfriend many times."

I kept my tone serious as I replied, "If your help has been invaluable, how will you put a figure on your invoice?"

She grinned. "I'm sure I could come up with a suitable amount. Where is Seb anyway? Didn't you say he's on a course or something?"

"Yes, some sort of course to do with the public perception about the police." I frowned. "Or something like that. There was a confusingly long title on the email he showed me about the course. It didn't make any sense to me. He's going to be away for two weeks."

"Let's hope there aren't going to be any murders soon. At least whilst he's away."

Her words made us fall silent for a few minutes.

"Well!" Peggy said loudly making me jump. "Let's keep ourselves busy whilst whatshername does whatever she's doing. I still think you should go up and see her. It's the polite thing to do."

"I'm not going up there. If you're so curious, you go."

"No chance. Anyway, this café could do with a good clean. I'll get the mop out."

We spent the next twenty minutes giving the café a clean which it didn't need.

We paused when we heard someone coming down the stairs.

A woman in her thirties was descending. She had the biggest smile on her face. Her face was alight with joy and her eyes were sparkling.

She headed straight for us and announced, "That was amazing! Truly amazing! I've had psychic readings before, but nothing like that. Wow! She was so accurate. And the things she said! She knows her stuff. Theodosia is the best psychic I've ever met. Thanks so much!"

Without any shame, Peggy asked, "What did she tell you?"

"Oh, I can't tell you that. It's private. Let me just say that she gave me some excellent advice. I know exactly what I need to do about a certain situation." Impossible as it seemed, her smile grew even more. She clasped her hands together. "I must go. Today is the first day of the rest of my life! Goodbye!"

She almost skipped as she crossed the floor and headed out of the door.

Peggy and I gave each other looks full of suspicion. I said, "Something doesn't feel right. How can someone be that happy over a reading? Or am I being overly suspicious?"

A steely look came into Peggy's eyes. She lifted her chin, threw her shoulders back, and said, "I'm going up there. I want to see what this marvellous psychic looks like."

A sudden trickle of fear went down my back. "Be careful. Don't get too close to her."

"I won't. I just want to see what she's like." She set off towards the stairs. She stopped and looked over her shoulder at me. "If I'm not back in ten minutes, come and get me."

"I will."

I didn't have to wait ten minutes. Peggy was back down in one minute. She said to me, "You have to get upstairs right now and see what's going on! You're not going to like it."

Chapter 3

P eggy refused to go with me, so I headed up the steps on my own. I
faltered halfway up because I got the familiar tingly feeling of an
approaching vision. I held the banister tightly and waited for the vision
to appear.

But nothing happened. The tingly feeling left me. Which was
weird.

I reached the top of the steps and stared in horror and confusion at
the scene ahead of me.

When we first opened the upstairs area of the café, it had been
designed as a relaxing place for our customers. There were the usual café
tables and chairs which we had downstairs, but we added a few sofas
that we placed next to the large windows which looked out over the
high street. To the rear of the room was a quieter reading area stocked
with many books that our kind customers had supplied.

The calm area wasn't like that now.

Our relaxing upstairs area had been converted into what I could
only describe as a boudoir. Swathes of purple material had been
festooned over the tables, sofas and bookcases. Incense sticks emitted
twirling flumes of scented smoke which made my nose tickle. The
customers who'd come upstairs were sitting cross-legged on a black
rug which was embellished with gold and silver stars. Their eyes were
closed, and they appeared to be deep in meditation. Or perhaps they
were thinking about their shopping needs for the upcoming week.
That's what always happened to me when I attempted to meditate.

But worse than that were the many, many candles which were dotted randomly around the room. There were so many that I could feel the heat coming off them. Our café had been turned into a fire hazard.

Anger rushed through me. I don't know who this Theodosia thought she was, but she was not going to cause my café to go up in flames!

I rushed over to the nearest bank of candles which were already dripping wax onto the purple fabric beneath them, and I blew them out. I moved on to the next collection of candles and extinguished them. Knowing I would need help to blow all the candles out before they set the room alight, I approached the people with closed eyes and said, "Hey, can I get some help here? Before we all go up in flames. These candles need to be extinguished. Right now!"

One man opened his eyes. "No can do, love. I'm meditating on my desires and intentions. That's what Theodosia asked us to do." He closed his eyes.

I prodded him on the shoulder. "You'll be meditating all the way to the hospital if you don't help me blow these candles out."

Keeping his eyes closed, he shook his head.

"Okay, fine!" I announced loudly. "In that case, I'm going to close the café immediately as a matter of emergency, and you'll all have to leave without seeing Theodosia. How does that sound?"

My words had the desired effect. Eyes sprang open and people quickly got to their feet. Within minutes, the offending candles had been dealt with. When the last candle had been put out, people gave me questioning looks. I nodded and said they could return to their meditating positions.

The man whom I'd first spoken to approached me. He said, "I've been waiting weeks for this reading. Theodosia hardly ever makes public appearances. She usually sees clients at her house, and her waiting list is ridiculous. I don't know how I managed to get an email inviting me here! That's not the sort of thing that happens to me. I never have good luck. Never. Born under an unlucky star, I was. Or under a curse."

Curiosity got the better of me. "How much does Theodosia charge?"

"Not enough by all accounts. I've heard nothing but amazing reports about her. Apparently, she can see right into your soul. You don't even have to speak. She knows what's troubling you, and how to fix it. I'll pay her whatever she asks me for after the reading."

"She asks you for money? She doesn't have a set amount?"

"Yeah, that's how it works. It depends on your problem. And my problem is enormous." He nodded sagely. "But not for much longer. My luck is going to change for the better. I can feel it."

I looked around the room. "Where is Theodosia?"

"Behind that curtain there. She's going to call us by name when she's ready for us. I hope I'm next. I probably won't be. Not with my luck."

All of a sudden, a female voice boomed out from behind the curtain, "I am ready."

"That's her!" the man exclaimed. "I hope it's me. I hope it's me."

There was a dramatic pause. The seated people opened their eyes and eagerly awaited the name of the person who was going to be called. Theodosia continued, "Karis Booth, I'm ready for you."

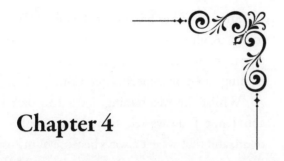

Chapter 4

I ignored the disgruntled looks coming my way from the seated meditators and moved towards the purple curtain where the disembodied voice had come from.

I pulled the curtain to one side and soon got my first look at Theodosia.

Thanks to the extra purple curtains which had been hung on the walls, the area I was now in was almost dark. I was suddenly wistful for a couple of candles. I squinted and made out a table right in front of me. There was an impressive crystal ball on the table, along with a few packs of illustrated cards and a variety of coloured crystals.

I thought I was alone until a woman slowly moved forward on the other side of the table. Somehow, by trickery or a hidden light, her face was illuminated. I could clearly see her flowing purple hair which cascaded over her shoulders. Her lilac eyes transfixed me with a piercing stare. Her bright red lips moved into a slow smile.

"Karis. Welcome. I've been expecting you." She opened her hand towards the chair in front of me which I'm certain hadn't been there a moment before. "Take a seat. I'm Theodosia. I'm a gifted psychic, amongst other things. I'm the seventh daughter of a seventh daughter."

"Right. Okay. Good." I didn't know what else to say. Everything seemed unreal. I had to remind myself I was upstairs in our friendly café and hadn't passed through into some enchanted land full of purple curtains. I slowly sat down without taking my eyes from Theodosia's lilac ones. She must be wearing contact lenses. Surely?

She waved her hand over the table. "What reading would you like today? A glimpse into the future via my crystal ball? A trip into the past from my selection of precious stones? Or perhaps you'd like a card reading based on a specific question?"

Whilst she was talking, I tried to pick up on any feelings I had about her. I always felt something about a new person when I met them, and that wasn't always because of my psychic abilities. Peggy and Erin were just the same. Peggy more so. She knew when someone was a 'rotten apple' within seconds of meeting them.

I continued to stare at Theodosia. But it was like I was looking at a brick wall. I didn't pick up on any feelings, good or bad. My thoughts were completely neutral, which was a worry because they never were when I met someone new.

"What's it to be, Karis?"

"I don't want a reading. I want to know who booked your event."

She gave me the slowest of nods. "All will be revealed in due course at the right time."

"I'd like you to reveal it now, please," I said as firmly as I could whilst withering slightly under her intimidating stare. "Was it my sister Erin? Or her husband Robbie? Did you phone or do it online?"

"The answers to those questions will be revealed soon enough." She tipped her head to one side. "Why did you douse my candles?"

"Because they were a fire hazard. There are lots of books up here. They could have set alight."

She gave me a condescending laugh. "Oh, Karis, don't be silly. Those candles would never have caused any such damage. I put a protective spell around them, a most powerful protective spell. They wouldn't have set fire to anything. I'd hardly leave a candle unattended without using a spell on it first. What kind of a gifted psychic do you think I am?"

My hackles rose. "Spell or not, I'd appreciate it if you didn't relight those candles. And no one gave you permission to put this fabric up everywhere."

"Or did they?" she asked enigmatically. "Perhaps the mystery person who gave me permission to be here also allowed me to decorate this area as I wanted."

"If you tell me who that was, then I could ask them."

She laughed. It held a hint of maliciousness. There was no mistaking it. "Let me give you a reading. Free of charge."

"No thanks." I folded my hands primly on my lap.

She pushed a pack of cards towards me. "Shuffle these."

"No."

"Okay. I'll do it for you." She continued to look at me intently as she shuffled the cards. Then she laid the top ones out in two rows of three.

I know I should have walked out before she started to speak, but I couldn't help myself from giving the cards a curious look.

Taking my silence as a sign I wanted her to continue, Theodosia examined the cards "Ah. Interesting. Very interesting."

"What is?" I immediately regretted my enthusiasm.

She tapped the card nearest her. "You're surrounded by a loving family. A supportive family. Which is good considering what's going to happen."

I sat up straighter. "What's going to happen?"

She tapped another card. "The loss of something important. Or someone important. It's not clear yet."

"What do you mean? Who? Give me a name." My voice rose in panic.

Theodosia frowned at the cards. "Just a moment. Let me think." She became silent. "Ah. Yes. Now I can see it clearly. You've already experienced the loss, but you're not aware of it yet."

"The loss of what?"

"Your gift. Your psychic gift. Karis, it's gone forever."

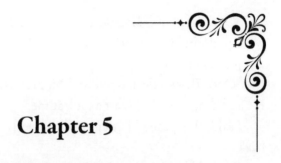

Chapter 5

I blinked at Theodosia, unable to speak.

She took advantage of my silence. "I apologise for delivering such bad news, but it had to be done. I feel your pain. To have such an amazing gift, and then to lose it must be causing you a great deal of anguish."

I still couldn't speak.

Theodosia carried on, "But all is not lost. I may be able to help you. For appropriate compensation, of course. I can't guarantee the return of your full abilities, but I may be able to bring something back which would be a relief to you, I'm sure. Here, take my card. I can see you're in shock. Understandably so. I would hate to be in your position." She pushed her card towards me.

Numbly, I took her card and stood up.

Theodosia made the mistake of smirking. That one movement caused my common sense to kick in. I said, "I don't believe you. Tell me who booked you. Tell me who you spoke to."

"No. It isn't time for you to know the answer yet. I'm sorry you don't believe me. You're in denial. Will you ask Montell Collins to come in?"

"I'm right here!" The man I'd spoken to earlier popped his head around the curtain. "Are you ready for me? Did you say my name? Or something that sounded like it? Probably the latter, knowing my luck."

"Are you Montell Collins?" Theodosia asked.

"Don't you know?" His face fell. "I thought you knew everything."

"Of course I do," Theodosia said with a dramatic roll of her eyes. "It was a philosophical question. Is Montell Collins *really* who you are? Or is it just an illusion?"

"Ooo. That's a deep question," Montell said. "Are you ready to give me a reading now?" He cast a look at me.

I said, "I'm going." I attempted to give Theodosia her business card back.

She held her hands up. "No. You're going to need it. Think about what I said, Karis Booth. Think very carefully."

I was thinking very carefully about what she said. And I was beginning to think she wasn't a nice person. And that was putting it mildly. She knew about my psychic abilities, but it wasn't exactly a secret. She could have found out somehow, and then decided to use that information against me.

I said calmly, "If you don't tell me who you spoke to about this event, then I have no option but to end it." I know I sounded stuffy and too official, but I couldn't help it.

Montell let out a heavy sigh. "This is all my fault. I take bad luck with me everywhere I go. I should have stayed at home."

Theodosia gave me a defiant stare. "I will not answer your question."

"Okay." I pushed the curtain to one side, stepped through, and was confronted by the hopeful looks coming from the cross-legged people. My heart sank. I couldn't turn them away, no matter how I felt about Theodosia. I would have to let the evening continue.

I went downstairs and found Peggy waiting for me.

"Well?" she asked. "Did you see what she had done upstairs? Those purple curtains? And all those candles? What a blooming nerve! Could have set the whole place on fire. I would have blown those candles out when I first saw them, but I wanted you to see them. Did you speak to whatshername? Did you give her a piece of your mind?"

"No. I need to tell you something." I took Peggy over to a table near the window. Once we were seated, I told her what Theodosia had said to me.

Peggy nearly exploded with rage. "She said what! How dare she? What does she know about anything? And she was going to charge you to get your psychic powers back? The ones you haven't even lost?" She pushed the sleeves of her cardigan up. "I'll go upstairs right now and have a word with her. I won't have anyone talking to you like that."

She made to rise, but I put my hand on her arm to stop her. "The thing is, she might be right. I haven't had any psychic visions for weeks now. What if I have lost my abilities? I almost had a vision earlier, but then it didn't happen." I thought of a suitable comparison. "It's a bit like when you're convinced you're going to sneeze and you get a tickly nose. But then you don't sneeze. Do you know what I mean?"

"I do. But your vision not happening doesn't mean anything. Does it?"

"I don't know." I looked at Theodosia's card. "But even if I have lost my gift, I wouldn't pay Theodosia to help me. There's something very devious and calculating about her. I don't trust her."

"Me neither, and I haven't even met her yet." Peggy looked towards the stairs. "Have you found out who booked her yet? Was it Erin or Robbie?"

"Theodosia wouldn't say. I'm beginning to think she didn't book it at all and just turned up. All I knew about her coming here was when I got that text from her a few hours ago to say she was on her way. I assumed someone else had confirmed everything with her. It's all very strange." I stood up. "I'm going to phone Erin again. If she confirms for certain she doesn't know anything about Theodosia, then I'm going to tell her to leave. I'll phone her from the kitchen."

"Good idea. If she doesn't go willingly, I'll help you." She pushed her sleeves up even higher.

I left the main café area and walked into the kitchen. As soon as I did so, the familiar tingly feeling came back to me.

I was about to get a vision.

Or was I?

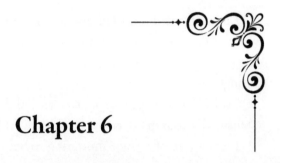

Chapter 6

I did get a vision.

I was no longer in the café's kitchen. I was sitting in an upholstered chair in an unfamiliar living room. I wasn't in my own body, but from looking down at myself, I had no idea whose body I was in other than it was female. That thought should have freaked me out, but it had happened to me many times before and I knew there was no need to panic.

I was looking at an open notebook on my lap. There was a list of names on one side, but as I focused on them, they became blurry. I looked at the other side of the page and saw a list of numbers. There were a lot of zeros. As soon as I focused on them, they too went out of focus.

A feeling of contentment and a job well done settled on me. I was feeling very proud of myself and of what I'd achieved.

A knock at the door sent a bolt of impatience through me. Now what? I didn't have any appointments booked. But I often got people turning up on the off-chance that I might give them a reading. I wasn't one to turn business away.

I stood up, left the room and stopped at the hallway mirror. I reached towards a set of drawers and pulled the top drawer open. I took out a purple wig and put it on. Once it was in place, I put my lilac contact lenses in. Satisfied I was ready, I checked my appearance in the mirror.

My reflection smiled back at me.

I opened the door. I felt a sense of familiarity as I looked at who was standing there. What were they doing back? Before I could ask that very question, I was struck heavily on the head. Searing pain shot through me.

"Why?" I managed to mutter as I slid to the carpet. The pain intensified. I couldn't open my eyes. My world turned black.

I was aware of a voice muttering something, but I couldn't make out the words.

"Why?" I muttered again. "Why?"

I felt someone roughly shaking me. I didn't respond. I couldn't. My breathing became shallow. I could feel my heartbeat slowing down. Death came closer.

I was aware I was in a vision, but I couldn't bring myself out of it.

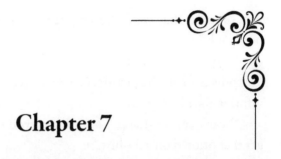

Chapter 7

"Karis! Come back to me. Don't die! Don't go towards the white light! Come back."

Someone was slapping my face. I opened my eyes and saw the concerned face of Peggy looming over me. She was the one who was slapping me.

"Ouch!" I put my hands up to stop her flailing hands. "Stop that. What am I doing on the floor?"

"Dying! That's what you're doing. Your face has gone all pale, and the life was draining right out of you. I saw it." Tears came to her eyes. "I thought you were a goner. I've been calling your name for ages! I've already phoned for an ambulance."

I sat up. "You'd better cancel that straight away."

She wiped a tear away. "No, I won't. You need to be checked over. You don't look good. A hair's breadth from death. I wish you wouldn't do this to me. It's not the first time."

"I feel fine. Honestly. I didn't mean to scare you. Cancel the ambulance. I don't want to waste their time. Please." I gave her a reassuring smile. "I'm okay. I promise."

She gave me a long look before saying, "Okay. I'll cancel it."

Whilst she was doing that, I tried to make sense of my vision. It didn't take me long to do so. By the time Peggy had finished her phone call, I was ready to talk about it. I gave Peggy the full details.

"It was Theodosia in my vision," I said. "As soon as I looked in the mirror, I could see it was her. I couldn't see who her assailant

21

was, though. They were blurred just like the figures and names in that notebook."

Peggy tutted. "I don't care much for your visions sometimes, Karis. You only get half the picture. Can't you get proper visions with all the information? Just once?"

"I can't control them. I keep telling you that. I think I'm going to get that printed on a T-shirt."

"Don't be flippant with me, young lady. You nearly died. If it wasn't for me slapping you around the face, you could have died. Then where would you be?"

I smiled. "Thank you for slapping me. I apologise for being flippant."

"I should think so." She pressed her lips together and looked at the ceiling.

I guessed her thoughts. "It was a premonition I had. It showed the future. Theodosia is going to be murdered."

She looked at me and nodded. "You have to tell her."

"She might already know. If she's that good a psychic, won't she already know?"

"She might not. But if you don't tell her, then what kind of a psychic does it make you?"

"A terrible one." I sighed as I got to my feet. "Okay. I'll tell her."

"I wonder how she'll take it?" Peggy asked.

I soon found out.

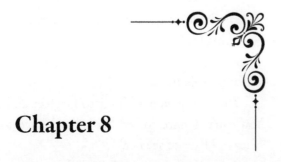

Chapter 8

As I left the kitchen, I saw Montell Collins heading towards the main café door. Like the woman I'd seen earlier who'd had a reading with Theodosia, he had a huge smile on his face.

He looked my way and said, "My luck has changed! Finally! Everything is going to be smoother sailing from now on. At last. I feel like a new man. And it's all thanks to that amazing woman upstairs. She's wonderful. Amazing. I'm so glad I came here today. That reading was worth every penny."

"What did she say to you?"

A guarded look crossed his face. "I don't know if I can talk about it. I don't want to jinx anything."

An instinct came to me. "Okay. Let me get the door for you." I moved in front of him, opened the door, and lightly put my hand on his elbow. As I did so, a fleeting vision came to me of Montell handing over a wad of cash to Theodosia. Goodness knows how much money it was but it looked like a lot.

Montell gave me a nod of farewell before leaving the café. Again, like the woman who'd left earlier, he had a spring in his step.

I went upstairs and looked at the people sitting on the floor. They all had their eyes closed in meditation. Keeping my steps light, I moved towards the curtain which divided the group from Theodosia. My movement caused a young woman with dark hair to open her eyes and give me a direct look.

"Where are you going?" she asked. "Are you pushing in?"

Everyone else opened their eyes. I almost wilted under their glowering looks.

I said, "I need to have an urgent word with Theodosia." I did a sideways walk like a crab.

The young woman leapt to her feet and dashed over to me. "No! You can't. I have to see her next. I have to." She touched my arm. "Please. I have to see her."

Another vision came to me. I was getting one after another now. The one this time concerned the woman in front of me. In my vision, I saw tears rolling down her face. But that wasn't the worst thing. I felt an overwhelming sense of despair which made my breath catch in my throat. It was followed by a painfully familiar emotion of betrayal. It was something I'd experienced many times during my marriage to my now ex-husband, Gavin.

I was so tempted to pull the young woman into my arms, but I resisted. It wasn't the sort of thing you did to a stranger.

My look softened. "I know you want to see her, and you will. But there is something I need to tell her. It is urgent. I hope you understand."

"How long will you be?"

I didn't speak for a moment because I wasn't sure how to answer her. How long did it take to tell someone they were going to be murdered? I settled on, "I'll be as quick as I can." I followed my words with a smile. "What's your name? Perhaps I can tell Theodosia to call you next."

"Would you? It's Verity Milligan." She gave me a wobbly smile. "Thank you."

"Do you know if there's anyone having a reading with Theodosia at the moment?"

"There's no one there. We're waiting for the next name to be called." She returned to her cross-legged position but didn't close her eyes.

I moved to the curtain and wondered if I should wiggle it or something to let Theodosia know I was there. Or should I call out to her?

I did neither. I pulled the curtain back and went over to the table where Theodosia was sitting with her eyes closed.

"Karis, you've come back." Her eyes opened. "I knew you would. I can read your mind. I know why you're here."

"Do you?" That would save me an awkward conversation. I sat down.

"Yes, you're here about your loss of powers. I can help you with your situation. It might take more than one session, but it'll be worth it. I can assure you of that." She wrote something on a piece of paper, folded it once, and pushed it towards me. "That's the initial consultation fee."

I ignored the paper. "I haven't lost my abilities. In fact, I've had three psychic visions since we last spoke."

She smiled smugly. "Have you really? Or do you just think you have? Are you trying to convince yourself?"

I ignored her tone. "I had a vision about you."

"I doubt that." She leaned back in her chair.

"I had a vision about you," I repeated. "You were sitting in your living room and looking at a notebook which had a variety of names and figures in it. You were feeling contentment, and you were proud of the job you'd done. It had something to do with the notebook."

Her smile vanished.

I went on, "There was a knock at your door. I saw you going into your hallway. You reached into a set of drawers and pulled out your wig." I pointed to her hair. "I saw you put it on. Then you put your lilac contact lenses in."

Theodosia blanched. She leaned forward on the table. "What else did you see?"

"You opened the door." I took a deep breath. "I didn't see who the person was, but you recognised them and wondered what they were doing back. Then...then they hit you. You fell down. I could feel the pain running through you. It was bad."

Her voice was not much more than a whisper now. "Did I die?"

I nodded. "It felt like that. You could have been knocked unconscious. I was brought out of my vision before I got the full picture."

Theodosia stared at the crystal ball in front of her as if seeing it for the first time. She blinked.

I stayed silent, waiting to see what she would say next.

"No," she said.

"No? No to what?"

"No to your vision. I don't believe you. You're making it up to convince yourself you haven't lost your gift."

"I'm not making it up," I said firmly.

"You must be. If I were to die soon, I would know about it. I would see it in my crystal ball. Or I would read it in my cards. I would feel it in my bones."

"Maybe psychics aren't able to predict their own deaths."

"Of course we are! Then we can prepare for them. I know many psychics who've seen their deaths. And I would have definitely foreseen mine if it was going to happen." She stood up. "Who are you tell me such lies? You're an evil woman. Evil."

I stood up too. "I'm not evil. And I'm not lying. How would I know about that notebook of yours? Or where you keep your wig?" I waved my hand dismissively. "I'm not going to defend myself. I've told you what I saw. It's up to you what you do with that information. There's a young woman who's keen to see you on the other side of your curtain. Her name is Verity Milligan. By the way, in another vision, I saw the cash Montell handed you. I don't know why they're giving you so much money."

Theodosia said tightly, "It's none of your business."

I walked away before I could retaliate. It was actually my business because it was taking place in the café, but I was well aware that she was helping the people who'd come to see her. I didn't want to interfere with that. I wasn't happy about it, though.

Peggy was waiting for me at the bottom of the steps. "Well? What did she say? Did she thank you?"

"No. She didn't thank me. She didn't believe me." I sighed. "But saying that, I can't leave things like this. I have to do something."

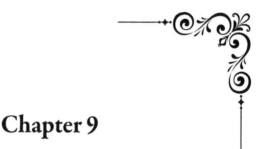

Chapter 9

"What can you do?" Peggy asked. "You've told her she's going to die, so it's up to her to do something now."

I shook my head. "But she thinks I'm lying." I relayed the conversation I'd had with Theodosia. Then I told Peggy about the visions I'd had with Montell and Verity.

Peggy asked, "Do you think they're related? The visions, I mean. Do you think one of them might be the killer? Did they have killer eyes?"

"I don't know what killer eyes look like. The visions could be related, though. Do we have a list of names for those people upstairs? Just in case?"

"Just in case one of them is a killer? I doubt we've got a list. We didn't even know this event was going ahead until you got that text from whatshername."

"Theodosia."

Peggy nodded. "Theodosia. I keep forgetting it. I should memorise it for when the police talk to us after she's been murdered."

"That's a bit harsh."

"Harsh, but true if your vision is to be believed. And I don't doubt that."

"Yes, but this is a premonition. We can stop it from happening." A thought came to me. "Seb! I'll phone him and let him know what's going on."

"And what will he do? Rush back from his conference and lock her in a cell?" She frowned. "Can he do that? For her own safety?"

"I don't think that's a possibility. But he could let me know who's dealing with things here in his absence. Perhaps I could have a word with them?"

Peggy's frown increased. "You'd have to tell them about your visions. Are you okay with that?"

"I'll have to be. Someone's life is in danger. I can't stand by and let something terrible happen."

"No, you can't. Is there anything I can do?"

I said, "You can phone Erin. I never got round to it earlier. Ask her again if she spoke to Theodosia about organising this event. She might even have a list of the attendees on the booking form. Hopefully."

"I'll interrogate her," Peggy replied. "In a kind but firm kind of way, of course. I'll take my call in the kitchen."

"And I'll take mine here."

I moved over to the window and sat at the table there. It was still light outside, and I stared out at the street. Some people were strolling along hand in hand. I noticed couples sitting in the Italian restaurant across the road. I realised how much I was missing Seb.

That was the first thing I told him when he answered my call. I followed it by saying, "I've had a premonition about someone dying. A possible murder. Can you lock a person up for their own safety?"

"Start at the beginning. Tell me everything."

Whilst I was giving Seb the full details, I noticed Peggy walking across the café. She gave me a little wave before heading upstairs. What was she up to?

Seb was saying something. I concentrated on his words. "My temporary replacement is DI Fiona Knox. She's fairly young, but comes highly recommended. I've never met her, and I don't know much about her."

"Should I talk to her? Tell her about my premonition?"

"I'm not sure that's a good idea. How to put this politely? We have a lot of people phoning us or coming into the office claiming to know the future and the crimes which are going to be committed. They also tell us when the world is going to end. There's a special file for them. I won't tell you what the file is called, and it's not me who named it."

"I can guess the name. I've been called many unsavoury names over the years. But don't you think it's worth getting in touch with DI Knox? She might understand my concerns."

"She might. And she might not." Seb paused. "Leave this with me. I'll talk to DI Knox and mention your concerns. I'll see what her response is. Will that help?"

"It might." I turned away from the window. "Perhaps I should have another word with Theodosia."

"You could. Apart from a possible impending murder, how are you? How's everyone else?"

Time flew by as I talked to Seb. He was so easy to talk to, and such a good listener too.

After a while, Seb said, "I'd better go. We've got some team-building thing starting in another room. They'll wonder where I've gone. We've been talking for thirty minutes."

"Have we?"

"We have. And I'd rather talk to you for another thirty minutes than converse with a load of strangers. But what can I do?"

I smiled. "You have to go and talk to strangers. I'll phone you later."

We ended the call. As I did so, I saw Peggy coming down the stairs. Something about her demeanour caused fear to grip me.

I was at her side in a flash. "Peggy? What's wrong?"

"Nothing. It's nothing." She averted her gaze and attempted to sidestep me. "I really should be getting home. I don't feel good. Can you manage on your own?"

"Peggy, look at me. What's happened? Why did you go upstairs?"

"It doesn't matter." She was still looking away from me. "There's a bus in ten minutes. I have to go."

"Peggy Marshall! Tell me what's going on?"

She finally looked at me. There were tears in her eyes. "I had a word with Erin about the booking. It was her who'd spoken to Theodosia, but it had completely slipped her mind. Theodosia just confirmed she'd spoken to Erin."

"And?"

"And what?"

"What else happened upstairs?" My eyes narrowed. "Did she say something to you?"

"She did." Peggy looked at her watch. "I should get a move on if I'm going to get that bus."

"What did she say to you? Peggy? She's upset you, hasn't she?"

"I don't want to talk about it. Karis, I can't talk about it. Not yet. Just let me be. Please." She moved away from me. "Will you be okay on your own? You will, won't you?"

"Of course. But why don't you wait and then I can give you a lift home?"

"I need to go now. I want to be alone." She didn't say another word as she collected her handbag and coat, and then left the café. It was so out of character for her.

What had Theodosia said to Peggy?

Chapter 10

I never did find out from Theodosia what she'd said to Peggy because three days later, the psychic was dead.

I found out about her demise from DI Fiona Knox who called in at the café the day after Theodosia had died.

It was in the afternoon and I was clearing up after the mothers and tots group. As much as I loved seeing the little ones, they made the most tremendous mess which took ages to clean up. I didn't mind because I knew how greatly the tired mothers appreciated the weekly meetings and the much-needed time to catch up with each other.

As I was sweeping up the last of the biscuit crumbs, a tall, slim woman in black jacket and trousers approached me and introduced herself.

"Good afternoon. I'm DI Knox. Do you have a moment?" Her tone was cold and businesslike.

"I do." I leaned the sweeping brush against the table.

"You are Karis Booth, is that correct?" She swiftly looked me over. "DCI Parker described you to me, and said I'd find you here at this time."

"I am Karis Booth. Is Seb okay? I spoke to him earlier, and he was fine then."

"This has nothing to do with DCI Parker. Well, that's not strictly true. He was the one who wanted me to tell you this news. Though what it's got to do with you, I don't know."

"What news?" I already had a feeling about what she was going to tell me. "Has it got something to do with a psychic called Theodosia?"

Her face was devoid of expression as she said, "It has. I regret to inform you that Theodosia Baker has passed away. It happened yesterday."

Even though I was expecting the news, the shock of it made my legs feel weak. I pulled out the nearest chair and sat down. "How did she die? Was she murdered?"

DI Knox sat next to me. "Why do you think she was murdered?"

Cautiously, I answered, "How much did Seb tell you about me?"

"He didn't tell me much, other than that you two are a couple, and that Ms Baker held an event here recently." Her face twisted in disgust. "He said it was a fortune-telling event or something like that. I hate all that nonsense. People taking advantage of the weak and vulnerable. They're no better than thieves. They should be locked up."

"Don't you believe in psychics then?"

"Absolutely not. How can someone predict the future? It's a load of rubbish. Don't tell me you believe in that stuff?"

"I do, actually. And so did all the people who came to Theodosia's event. Can you tell me more about her death?"

"I can tell you as much as DCI Parker thinks you should know. She was found dead in her home with a suspected blow to the head."

"A suspected blow? Don't you know if she was hit for certain? Wasn't there an injury? Blood? Bruises?"

DI Knox got to her feet. "That's all I'm prepared to tell you. I've done what DCI Parker asked of me."

"Don't you want to know about the event here? Who was here, and what Theodosia said to them?"

"Why would I want to know that?"

"Because they could be murder suspects." I clamped my mouth shut but I already knew I'd gone too far.

Her eyes narrowed. "What is it with you and murder? Are you one of those middle-aged women who watch crime shows all the time and now consider yourself an expert when someone dies?"

"No, it's not that at all. Forget I said anything." I stood up and took hold of the sweeping brush. "Do you want to leave me your card?"

"Why would I do that? I doubt we'll be speaking to each other again."

Unable to stop myself, I blurted out, "Do you suspect foul play? If Theodosia received a blow to the head, someone must have done that, and does that mean foul play was involved?"

For a moment, she looked as if she wasn't going to answer me. "If you must know, Ms Booth, Theodosia was most likely involved in a robbery which went wrong."

I stopped myself from rolling my eyes. I'd heard that reason used before in other murders I'd unwittingly become involved in. I wisely kept quiet.

DI Knox continued, "There have been robberies around that area for the last few days. It appears the thief wasn't expecting Ms Baker to be at home when they broke into her property. She must have disturbed the thief."

"Where was she in the house when she died?"

"That's none of your business."

If my premonition had come true, then Theodosia would have died whilst answering the door to someone. If she had died at the front door, then how could the police think it was a robbery gone wrong? The thief would hardly knock at the door? Would they? Or is that how some criminals worked? Knocked at the door first to see if anyone was in?

These were questions which I couldn't ask DI Knox. If Seb were dealing with the case, then I would have fired one question after another at him.

Seb! I wondered if he could tell me anything about Theodosia.

I could try. I was going to phone him anyway.

But before I phoned him, there was someone else I wanted to talk to.

Someone who was causing me a lot of distress, and I didn't know what to do about her.

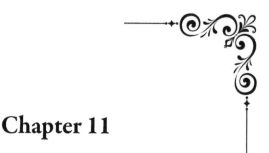

Chapter 11

Not long after my conversation with DI Knox, I found Peggy sitting in her living room with the curtains half closed. I had let myself in using the spare keys she'd given my mum years ago. Peggy also had a set of keys for Mum's house next door, the house I was currently living in. It was a comfort to have Peggy so close, especially at a time like this when she needed a lot of attention.

"It's only me," I said unnecessarily as I walked over to Peggy. She was staring at a framed photo of her late husband, Jeff. Since leaving the café on the night of Theodosia's event, Peggy hadn't been herself. She'd taken to sitting in her armchair in the semi-darkness, often with that framed photo in her hands.

"Hello, love," she replied quietly. She didn't take her attention off the photo. She looked as if she were expecting Jeff to answer an unspoken question.

I was shocked at her appearance but didn't say anything. I'd called in every day since the event at the café and made sure she'd eaten and slept. I'd seen her the previous evening and sat with her whilst we had a takeaway, which she'd only picked at. But her appearance had changed in that short time. Even in the half-light, I could see how sallow her skin was, and how exhausted she looked.

I knelt at the side of the armchair. I said gently, "Peggy, did you sleep last night? Have you eaten today?"

She blinked and turned her head away from the photo. "Karis? When did you get here?"

"Just now. Peggy, I'm going to make you a cup of tea. And then we're going to talk about Theodosia and what she said to you."

"Oh, no. I can't tell you. Theodosia told me not to tell anyone. It's private."

I said, "I've had a visit from the police."

"Seb?"

"No, not Seb. He's on a course, remember?"

"Is he?"

"Yes. It was someone else who talked to me. A woman called DI Knox. Peggy, Theodosia is dead. She died yesterday."

"Dead? What do you mean?"

"Dead. Erm...as in dead. No longer alive."

"She's dead?" Peggy stared at the curtains. "Dead?"

"Yes. And that means you can now tell me what she said to you."

Peggy turned her head and looked at me. "I don't think I can. It's too sad."

"Try. Please. I'm worried about you."

She gave the photo to me. "Okay. I suppose I can tell you now. She said something about my Jeff."

I smiled at the photo. Jeff had adored Peggy. She was the centre of his world.

"What did she say?" I asked.

Peggy swallowed. "She said he didn't love me as much as I loved him."

"What?"

"That's what she said." Her voice trembled as she continued, "She said he had other women during the time we were together. A lot of women." A solitary tear trickled down her cheek.

A wave of hot anger rushed through me. It was hard to keep my voice steady. "She said that? About your lovely Jeff?"

"She did."

"And you believed her?"

"I did. She was very convincing. I knew she was telling me the truth because she knew other things about me."

"Like what?"

"She knew I worked at the café."

"Is that all?" I asked. "She could have worked that out."

"She knew I was outside the curtain waiting to speak to her."

I frowned. "She knew the same about me when I was waiting. She probably has a secret camera set up to keep an eye on anyone who was nearby. Did she say anything else about Jeff?"

"Not much. She did say I could have a formal session with her. She would contact Jeff and get some more details for me. She gave me her card. She said she'd charge appropriately depending on how difficult it would be to contact Jeff in the afterlife."

I was so angry that I didn't trust myself to speak.

All of a sudden, a very peculiar feeling came over me.

It was like someone was trying to invade my thoughts. Like someone invisible was whispering in my ear. I couldn't make out what the words were, though. It was like a dull static, the kind you get as you're trying to tune to a radio station. I instinctively knew the words were going to become clearer any second, and that frightened me.

I put my hands over my ears as if that would help.

It didn't.

The static lessened, and my fear increased.

Peggy gave me a concerned look. "Karis? What's wrong? Have you got earache?"

I took my hands from my ears. "Someone's trying to take over my mind. I think they're trying to give me a message."

"It'll be Theodosia. She's communicating from the spirit world. Is she angry with me? She told me not to talk about our conversation. I knew I shouldn't have said anything to you." Peggy turned away from me. "You'd better leave before she puts a curse on me from the afterlife."

"Peggy, you're being ridiculous." I cringed as the horrible feeling inside my head intensified. "If it is Theodosia trying to talk to me, she can clear off!"

With those words, the invading voice vanished.

I tried to tell Peggy the voice had gone, but my dear friend looked like she'd gone into a trance. She was staring unseeingly at the wall in a way which sent shivers down my spine. It reminded me of the way Mum stared out of the window at the care home she was living in. Fresh anger about Theodosia rose in me.

I put the framed photo of Jeff back on Peggy's lap. I said softly, "I'm going to sort this out, somehow. I'll find out who killed Theodosia, and I'll prove that Jeff was nothing like the man she claimed he was." Before leaving, I kissed her on the cheek and told her I'd check on her later.

All I had to do now was talk to people who had a grudge against Theodosia. I suspected she had many. How was I going to find them all?

Chapter 12

The sound of crying met me as I walked into Erin and Robbie's house later. For a moment, I thought it was the parents who were crying. But then I recognised the high-pitched wail that can only come from a baby. Or two babies in this case.

Erin and Robbie were sitting on the sofa with a crying infant in each of their arms. The grown-up faces were pale apart from the purple circles under their eyes. The babies, on the other hand, looked robust and full of vitality as they cried their little hearts out.

Erin cast me a look laden with despair. "They won't stop crying. We've fed them. Changed them. Sung one annoying lullaby after another. We even took them for a drive in the car. But they won't stop. We're terrible parents."

Robbie nodded. "We are. Just terrible. We don't know how to get them to stop."

As if agreeing, little Maggie and Charlie ramped up the volume of their cries. Erin began to cry too, though not as loudly.

"You are not terrible parents," I said as I moved over to the exhausted pair. "Sometimes, babies cry for unknown reasons. Let me have Maggie." I took the baby from Erin's arms. I smiled and rocked her gently. "Now then, little one, what's going on? Why are you making such a racket? Hmm? Look at what you're doing to your parents."

Maggie's wails reduced in volume.

Erin whispered to me, "Keep talking to her. Don't stop." She yawned and closed her eyes.

"Take mine," Robbie pleaded. He lifted Charlie. "Please. I'll pay you a thousand pounds to take him."

"I've got my arms full. Just a moment." I placed Maggie in the cot which had been set up in the living room. She had stopped crying altogether by now. I took Charlie from Robbie, and then placed him next to his sister. The cheeky scamp stopped crying as soon as I lay him down. I didn't know if it was my imagination, but I could have sworn I saw a twinkle in the babies' eyes.

Loud snores erupted from behind me. Erin and Robbie had fallen asleep within seconds. Erin was snoring louder than her husband, but I would never tell her that.

I pulled a chair up next to the twins and looked at them. Their chubby faces plucked at my heartstrings. They were so beautiful.

"Now then, you two," I said quietly, "what are you doing? Your poor parents are exhausted. They're not going to be any fun in that state, are they? Your lovely mother will be too tired to do any baking. She hasn't done any for weeks. You don't know this yet, but she makes the best cakes in the world. And I, for one, am missing them. So, if you don't mind, could you keep your crying to a minimum? Let your mother have a rest."

Maggie regarded me solemnly. Charlie emitted a burp.

I carried on talking, "As for your father, I don't know where to begin with him. He's one of the nicest people I've ever met. Always cheerful. Always knows what to do in a crisis. And he's wonderful at DIY. Not to sound selfish, but I've got a few jobs lined up for him at home. I could do them myself, but your father has already said he'd do them. But he can't if he's exhausted, can he? So, if you don't mind too much, can you stop making such a fuss? We all love you so much, and you're constantly in our thoughts. Unnecessary crying is not needed to get any more attention from us. What do you say? Will you stop crying so much?"

Charlie let out another burp. I assumed it was a burp of agreement. Maggie yawned.

"There's one more thing," I said. "I'm worried about Peggy. You know Peggy, don't you? She absolutely dotes on the pair of you. She's not very well in her mind. I have some work to do which might help her. I need some information, and I'm hoping very much I'll find that information on your mother's computer. I'm going to look for it now, and I'll sit right here whilst I do that. If you need a cuddle or a nappy change, just let me know. Okay? If you want to have a sleep, go ahead."

Maggie's little eyes were already closing. Charlie started to yawn. To help them on their journey into the land of Nod, I softly sang them a lullaby. It was one I used to sing to my daughter Lorrie. It never failed then, and it didn't fail me now. The twins were soon asleep. I felt like a superhero.

As carefully and slowly as if walking through a dynamite-strewn room, I walked over to where Erin's laptop was. Silently, and as stealthily as the experienced spy I'd suddenly assumed myself to be, I returned to my seat next to the cot and opened up the machine.

I was hoping Erin had a list of the people who'd attended Theodosia's event at our café. It would be super helpful if she had their email addresses, or even their actual addresses.

The logical side of my brain said I was a naïve idiot for thinking such things. But my newly acquired superhero status thought otherwise.

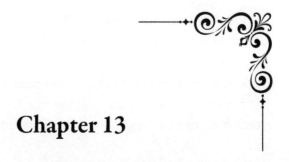

Chapter 13

Ten minutes later, I punched the air and mouthed "Yay!" Erin had made an entry about Theodosia's event, but it hadn't been on the café's website. I'd found it under a list of possible schools for the twins which had piqued my interest whilst scrolling through Erin's files. The list included pros and cons for each school. I got lost for a few minutes in Erin's reasoning for each school, but going by the nonsensical words she'd used, I assumed she'd been half asleep when she'd written those reasons.

The entry concerning Theodosia's event, which was listed under the last school, included the names of people who had confirmed their attendance be emailed to Theodosia. Each name had a number next to it. Their emails were included, and their home addresses too. I could not believe my luck. Why had Theodosia given those details to Erin? Oh. Maybe she really had known about her death, and that it wouldn't be classed as a murder. Maybe she'd known I'd be looking into her death. The thought made me shudder.

I gave the list a sideways glance, suddenly suspicious of how easy this was. If Theodosia had known about her future demise, couldn't she have done something to prevent it? Or had she considered it her destiny and something which couldn't be changed?

Did she speak to her killer the night of her event? And had she known she was speaking to her killer at the time? Wow. That was a scary thought.

I looked at the list of names. There were twelve. If Theodosia had known who was going to kill her, could she have made a note about it somehow? Some cryptic message in this list? But maybe there had been more than one person who had the intention of killing her. More than one person who had a grudge against her. Considering how her cruel words had effected Peggy, I could understand why people didn't like her.

My heart sank at the thought of Peggy. How could she believe such lies? I was certain they were lies, and Theodosia had told them just to get money out of Peggy in the resulting charade of contacting Jeff in the afterlife.

I looked at the list again, hoping some names would helpfully jump out at me. None did. I sent a copy of the list to my phone. Maybe something would jump out at me when I next looked at it.

I was about to close the file when I spotted something about how the names were ordered. Was this the order in which Theodosia had given readings to them?

I recalled the first woman who'd had a reading. According to the list, her name was Bonita Stevens. She didn't live that far away. She'd seemed ecstatic after her reading. I had a strong feeling that I should contact her, preferably in person. But what excuse could I use to talk to her?

I wasn't sure, but I would think of something on the way. Apprehension filled me as I realised I shouldn't be doing this, and I should let the police know about this list. But they didn't consider Theodosia's death a murder and probably wouldn't do anything. And I didn't relish the idea of talking to DI Knox again. But I couldn't sit back and do nothing.

Once again, my thoughts went to Seb. If he were dealing with this case, then I wouldn't feel so bad about calling on Bonita Stevens. I was tempted to phone him, but he'd only tell me to leave it alone. Or maybe he wouldn't. Knowing how much I'd helped the police in the past when

I should have left things alone surely would convince him I was doing the right thing. Surely?

I nodded to convince myself I was doing the right thing. I further justified my impending action by thinking I was doing this to support a fellow psychic who'd met an untimely death. Even if I hadn't liked her very much.

Looking back at the list, I saw a name I recognised. It was Montell Collins, the man who'd been convinced his luck had been changed by Theodosia. I could talk to him too and see if that was the case. I could lie and say it was a follow-up service which we'd started to offer.

That young woman, the one who'd been betrayed. What was her name? I scanned the list. Ah, there it was. Verity Milligan. I could talk to her and see how she was doing. She'd been upset before the reading, and I was genuinely interested to see how things had gone for her.

That was three people I could visit. It was a start.

Maybe none of them had anything to do with Theodosia's death, but they might be able to give me some helpful information.

I stayed where I was for a short while until Erin finally stirred and woke up. I pointed to the sleeping twins. I mouthed, "I have to go."

Erin sat up straighter and put her hands over her heart. She whispered, "Don't leave. Stay here forever. I need to sleep. For weeks and weeks. You have the magic touch. Please, don't go."

"I have to," I whispered back. "You'll be fine. These sleepless times don't last forever. I'll come back later."

As I stood up, she grabbed my arm. "Don't go," she quietly pleaded.

"You'll be fine." I pulled my arm free, kissed her on the head, and made my escape.

Chapter 14

When Bonita Stevens answered the door to me, I was taken aback at her appearance. She had the same look of hopelessness which Peggy had on her face. She also looked as if she hadn't slept for days.

"Yes?" she asked as she held the door partly closed. She followed this with a frown. "Do I know you?"

"Yes, we met the other night. At the café. You had a reading with Theodosia. We had a brief chat. You looked happy about your reading." She didn't look the slightest bit happy now.

Her eyes watered. "Right. Yes. I remember."

Keeping my tone bright and cheerful so that my lies would sound more convincing, I said, "We offer a follow-up service after each event we hold at the café. I could have sent an email, but I think a personal visit is, well, more personal. Would you mind sparing me a few minutes of your time? I'd like to know how your experience of the event was."

She burst into tears and held on tightly to the door. She looked like she was going to collapse, so I rushed forward and grabbed her.

Her tears became more hysterical, so still holding her, I stepped into her house. We were in the kitchen. I helped her over to the nearest chair. She sat down heavily and put her head in her hands as she continued to cry. I sat next to her and ineffectively patted her back. Should I make a cup of tea? That was always the first thing I did in an emergency. I glanced around the kitchen looking for the kettle.

Bonita suddenly stopped crying. She lifted her head, wiped her wet cheeks, and said, "I wish I'd never set eyes on Theodosia. I wish she were dead!"

This was awkward.

Should I be the one to tell her?

I reckoned she would find out soon enough, so I might as well be the one to tell her.

"She is dead," I said as respectfully as I could.

"Who?"

"Theodosia. She's dead."

"She is? When?"

"Yesterday. I had a visit from the police. They told me about her."

Bonita leaned back in her chair, her unhappiness replaced with shock. "Blimey. Did they say how she died? Was it a suspicious death?"

"Why are you asking that?"

She shrugged. "I imagine she made lots of enemies. I'll be honest, she made one of me." She stood up. "Would you like a cup of tea? I need one."

"Yes. Thank you."

She moved over to the kettle. "Would you like to know what Theodosia said to me? And what she made me do?"

I tried not to sound too eager. "Yes. If you don't mind."

Bonita made two very strong cups of tea. Mine was very dark brown, but I didn't complain. She provided a plate of biscuits to go with the tea. She ate three in quick succession as if trying to eat her feelings. I politely ate one and waited for her to start talking.

Once she'd finished the last biscuit and wiped crumbs from her mouth, she explained, "I work in a human resources department in a large office in Leeds. It's for a sales company. I've worked there for over fifteen years and I've seen the workforce get younger and younger every year."

I nodded at that.

She continued, "There are always strong characters in every business, those who stand out. They who are born leaders and always full of confidence. They almost seem to shine with their brilliance. Do you know what I mean? Have you ever met anyone like that?"

I nodded again. My ex-husband had been full of confidence and self-assurance. He had confidently lied to me for years about the affairs he'd had.

"Rafferty Palmer," Bonita said. "Everyone calls him Raff. He's the man who stands out at the office. One of the leaders. One of the go-getters. And handsome too. You couldn't help but notice him. He was in my department often because he had a high turnover of staff due to the nature of his job."

"What do you mean?"

"Raff had lots of targets to meet, and his staff didn't always provide the results he wanted. He'd give them warnings to get them to improve, but that didn't always work out the way he wanted and he'd often had to remove people who weren't performing well. So, he needed a steady influx of new staff. Which meant we had to spend a lot of time together. Even though he's ten years younger than me, we got on really well. Everyone called him cold-hearted, and a bit of a bully, but I didn't see that. I saw a caring side to him." She sighed. "I think you can guess where this is going."

"You fell for him."

She nodded. "I did. Big time. I looked forward to him getting rid of staff because then he would come into my office and talk to me about hiring a new batch of people."

I couldn't help myself from saying, "That seems harsh. People kept losing their jobs, and you looked forward to that?"

"I did. Looking back now, I can see how awful that sounds. I couldn't see it at the time." She smiled softly. "I knew how I felt about him, but I didn't know if he felt the same. He'd give me these long looks sometimes, as if he liked me, but he never said anything. I was having sleepless nights because I couldn't stop thinking about him. I had to find out one way or another if he liked me."

"Is that what you talked to Theodosia about?" I asked.

"I did." Her eyes turned steely. "She gave me some advice. Some terrible advice."

"What did she say?"

"She said Raff was definitely in love with me but was too shy to make a move. He'd been waiting for me to make the first move, for me to say something to him."

I asked, "Did you believe her?"

"Not at first, but she was very persuasive. She said I was the love of Raff's life, and he couldn't stop thinking about me. She said I had to be brave and take control, show him what a powerful woman I was. He would admire that. That's what she said anyway. She suggested a public display of my love would be the best way forward."

"She did? How did you feel about that?"

"Scared. But Theodosia was adamant Raff was waiting for me to do something like that. By the time I left your café, I was ready to take control."

A sense of foreboding went through me. I wasn't sure I wanted to know what happened next.

Bonita shoved another biscuit into her mouth and crunched on it noisily as if taking her anger out on it.

I waited for her to speak.

She swallowed the biscuit. "The next day at work, I gathered all my courage and went down to the sales floor. I knew Raff was having a sales pep talk with his team. He did that every day at the same time. I knew he'd have an audience."

"Oh no." I inwardly cringed.

"I marched into that meeting with my head held high. I'd put my best clothes on, my highest heels which I could hardly walk in, and some bright red lipstick which had come free with a magazine I'd bought months ago. I felt powerful and strong, full of confidence."

I cringed some more.

"Raff was in full swing when I walked onto the sales floor. I marched right up to him. He stopped talking. Everyone on the floor stared at me. Even those who weren't part of Raff's team stopped what they were doing and gawped at me. It was like they were collectively holding their breaths as they waited to hear what I was going to say." She stopped talking, her eyes widening as she remembered what had happened.

"What did you say?" I prompted her.

"I had planned to say that I liked and admired him, but instead, I blurted out that I loved him."

"Oh no."

She said, "It gets worse. I said that I knew he felt the same, and it's time we stopped wasting time and got together. As soon as I said those words, a horrible cold feeling went over me. The cold truth of realisation. Raff stared and stared at me like he couldn't believe what was happening. Then he started laughing. He asked if everyone else was hearing what he was hearing. Everybody started laughing then. Some people were recording me on their phones. I wanted the ground to swallow me up. I've never been so mortified in my life. But it got even worse."

"How?"

"Raff started to insult me. He called me old. Ugly. Stuck-up. Boring. Each insult felt like an arrow in my heart. He said he wouldn't go out with me if I were the last woman on the earth. I was too horrified to move for a while, but when he started to film my discomfort on his phone, I finally moved. I turned around and fled from that room. The laughter followed me all the way back to my office. I couldn't stay in my office, though. I collected my things and left work. I haven't been back since. I told them I'm ill but they must know I'm lying because the videos of me proclaiming my love to Raff are all over the internet."

"You poor thing. What a horrible thing to happen." I remembered the business card which Theodosia had given me. Maybe she gave one to Bonita too. "You must have blamed Theodosia for this. And quite rightly too. Did you contact her afterwards?"

Bonita's look turned evasive. "No. I thought about it, but what was the point? What's done is done. I should have trusted my instincts when she first told me Raff was in love with me. It's my own fault for listening to her." She stood up and took her cup over to the sink. With her back to me, she said, "So, there you have it. Is there anything else you want to know?"

I did want to know if she'd gone to see Theodosia at her home and bashed her on the head. But I didn't ask her that.

I asked, "Will you return to work?"

"I'll have to. I've got bills to pay." She turned around. "At least I'm not thinking about Raff all day anymore. I am having nightmares about what happened, but not many, because I'm not sleeping." She walked over to the kitchen door and opened it. "Thanks for listening to me. If you don't mind, I've got things to do."

I gave her a small smile before saying goodbye and leaving.

As I drove away, I saw her looking out of the window at me. It made me wonder if Bonita Stevens was the one who'd killed Theodosia.

Chapter 15

I did plan to visit Montell Collins next to see how his luck had
changed, and what Theodosia had said to him. But as I drove along,
Peggy's face kept coming into my mind. Not her normally happy face,
but her sad one. It made my heart ache. I had to do something about
her, and do something now.

I changed direction, and it wasn't long before I was back in Peggy's
living room. She was sitting in the same chair, and the curtains were still
half closed. She was looking at a photograph album this time. When I
got closer, I saw it contained Peggy and Jeff's wedding photos. In the
photos, he was gazing at his new wife as if he couldn't believe his good
luck.

"Hey, Peggy," I said as I crouched at her side. "Those are lovely
photos."

"It's all a lie. All of it. That look on his face. Those vows he made.
He didn't mean any of it."

The feeling of someone trying to get into my mind came back to
me. It was even stronger this time, but it no longer scared me.

I gently took the photograph album from Peggy. I put it on the
carpet. I took Peggy's hands in mine. "Peggy, do you remember when
I was last here? And I said someone was trying to communicate with
me?"

She nodded. "It was Theodosia."

"It wasn't. But I know who it is now. Before I tell you that, I have to
ask you something."

"Okay."

I looked into her eyes. The eyes I knew so well. "Do you really believe what Theodosia told you about Jeff?"

She didn't answer me.

"Look into your heart. Think about Jeff and your life together. How he talked to you. How he looked at you." I smiled. "I remember clearly how he looked at you. But I want to know how you feel. How you truly feel about him."

Peggy's face softened. "I loved him. I still do. I think about him every day."

"I know that, but what about Jeff? How do you think he felt about you?"

A slow smile came to her face. "He loved me. Truly loved me. He told me that every single day. It was the first thing he said on a morning, and the last thing he said at night. Even when we'd had arguments, he would tell me he loved me, and then our argument would be forgotten."

"Do you really believe what Theodosia said about him?"

She considered my question for a full minute. "No. I don't." Her nose wrinkled. "But why would she say those things unless she thought they were true?"

"Because she was trying to con you into giving her money at a later date. Peggy, I know who's been trying to get into my head."

Peggy bristled, looking more like her normal self. "I hope it is Theodosia. I want to give her a piece of my mind."

"It's not her." I took a deep breath. "It's Jeff. He wants to talk to you."

Chapter 16

I heard Jeff's voice in my head. A voice I remembered so well. It was like he was standing very close to me and talking into both ears at the same time. So strong was his voice, it was hard for me to find my own thoughts.

Jeff's words came out in a tumble into my mind. I held my hand up. "Whoa! Jeff! Slow down. I can't make sense of what you're saying."

Peggy stared at me. "Is it really him? My Jeff? Karis, you're not messing about are you?"

Jeff's words filled my head. I winced and waved my hands trying to get him to stop. I managed to yell, "Jeff! Please! Slow down."

Peggy cried out, "Jeff! If that is you, take a deep breath and calm down. If you can take a breath, that is. Look at what you're doing to poor Karis."

Jeff's words became less jumbled. It was like slowing down the playback facility on a recording. "Sorry about that, Karis love," he said. "I've been trying to get through for ages, ever since that horrible woman upset my Peggy. Can you hear me better now?"

I nodded, then realised he might not be able to see me doing that. I didn't know how these things worked. I'd never had a deceased person talking to me before. Was deceased even the right word? Jeff sounded just like his old self.

I said, "I can hear you clearly, Jeff. What do you want to say?"

Peggy sat forward on her seat. "Is it him? What's he saying? Tell me. Tell him I miss him. I miss him so much. Every day."

Jeff chuckled. "I know she misses me. I miss her too, my little Pickle-Peg."

I repeated Jeff's words which resulted in Peggy bursting into tears. In between sobs, she muttered, "Pickle-Peg. Pickle-Peg! It is my Jeff."

"Pickle-Peg?" I asked.

Jeff explained, "We had pickles in our sandwiches on our first date. I hated the things, but Peggy loves them. She ate all of mine, and hers too. Because she loved them so much, I'd always order extra whenever they were on the menu."

"What's he saying now?" Peggy asked between sobs. "Something romantic?"

"He's telling me about your nickname."

Peggy snorted. "Him and his nicknames. That's not the only one he used over the years." Her sobs were replaced with chuckles. A blush came to her cheeks. "I hope he doesn't tell you some of his others."

"I hope so too," I replied somewhat stiffly. "Jeff, do you want to talk to Peggy about Theodosia?"

Jeff swore profusely which made me grimace. Then he said, "I don't need to tell Peggy it was a pack of lies. I heard what she just said about not believing that woman. The only reason that fortune teller said those lies was to upset Peggy, and then get money from her in the future. She's done it with other people. She preys on their vulnerabilities. She picked up on how much Peggy was missing me."

"Let me just tell Peggy that." I relayed his comments to Peggy. She swore just as profusely as Jeff had done.

Jeff continued, "That woman was a psychic, I'll give her that much. But she used her talents for evil. To get money. And sometimes she upset people just for a twisted sense of fun."

"How do you know this?" I asked.

He replied, "I was with Peggy when she spoke to Theodosia. I picked up on that woman's thoughts, and I saw some of her memories. It didn't last long, but it was long enough to know what sort of a person she was. I was furious about what she was telling my Pickle-Peg! How dare she?" He added a few more curse words. I didn't know he had such a wide vocabulary.

"What's he saying now?" Peggy asked.

Once again, I repeated his words but missing out the swearing.

Peggy tutted and shook her head. "That woman! Ask Jeff if he knows who killed her."

"Jeff? I'm assuming you can hear Peggy?"

"I can" he answered. "Can you tell her she looks even more beautiful today than when I first met her?"

"In a moment. Do you know who killed Theodosia?" If he did know, how was I going to repeat that to DI Knox? I didn't suppose people from the spirit world could be reliable witnesses.

"I don't know who killed her," Jeff said. "Unfortunately. But I do know she was murdered. I could see it hanging in the air above her like a red mist. I could also feel the hate which people had for her. There was a lot of it."

In a hopeful tone, I asked, "Did that hate come from any of the people who were waiting to have a reading? Those people in the café?"

"I've no idea, Karis. Sorry. I've not done this sort of thing before. I didn't know what I was looking out for. I've kept an eye on Peggy and your family from afar, but I've never come this close to contacting someone before. But I had to do something. I couldn't see my Pickle-Peg looking so sad."

I repeated his words. I asked him some more questions about Theodosia, but he had nothing more to tell me. After I'd exhausted every avenue I could think of about Theodosia, I asked Jeff if he'd like to talk to Peggy about anything else.

I added firmly, "Keep it clean. And swear-free, if you don't mind."

Peggy laughed at that. "He was quite the potty-mouth, my Jeff. He made me blush sometimes."

"He made *you* blush?" I asked. "That must have taken some doing."

I spent the next ten minutes repeating Jeff's words to Peggy. There were many slushy comments, but then Peggy asked him where he'd put the large hammer with the wonky handle, and should she replace a section of fence at the bottom of the garden or just get it repainted.

Jeff's voice became fainter and fainter, and I found it harder to make out his words. I could feel him slipping away. It made me feel incredibly sad.

When I'd asked Jeff to repeat his latest words for the fifth time because I couldn't hear them properly, Peggy said, "Let him go, Karis. It's time. Jeff, I love you with all my heart. I always will. Thank you for talking to me and Karis. I'll see you when it's my time." She blew a kiss into the air.

Jeff's parting words were full of love and adoration for his wife. Tears were running freely down my cheeks as I repeated them to Peggy. Her tears flowed just as profusely as mine.

Jeff left my head completely. Peggy and I reached for the tissues and gave our noses a big blow.

In a determined manner, Peggy said, "Right. Let's find out who murdered that horrible woman. I do feel like we should congratulate whoever it was, but that's just my anger talking. Are you ready to go now?"

"Go where?"

"I'm assuming you've got some leads to follow up on. You should have by now unless you've been faffing about doing something else. Give me a minute whilst I get my coat."

I smiled as she left the room. It was good to have her back.

Chapter 17

After telling Peggy about the list of names I'd found on Erin's computer, we headed to Montell Collins' home. On the drive there, I told Peggy about my talk with Bonita Stevens, and how she'd made a fool of herself in front of her love interest.

"The poor girl. But she'll get over it. We've all made a fool of ourselves in the name of love." She peered through the windscreen. "Is this the right street? All the houses are boarded up. I'm presuming they're empty. They look like they're going to be pulled down soon."

"It is the right address. We're looking for number forty-eight Paradise Road. It's down this way."

We drove past one dilapidated house after another. Some of them had demolition notices on their doors.

"I wouldn't like to live on a street like this," Peggy pointed out. "Paradise Road! It looks nothing like I've imagined Paradise to look like. What sort of an idiot would want to stay here?"

We soon find out what kind of an idiot would stay there. Montell Collins was standing outside the door of number forty-eight. His arms were folded, and his face flushed with anger. He was arguing with a suited man holding a clipboard.

"I'm not going anywhere, I tell you!" Montell shouted, his words coming loudly and clearly through the closed windows of my car. "I won't be moved. You can shove those demolition notices where the sun doesn't shine!"

We stopped a few doors up and got out of the car. The man with the clipboard was trying to say something, but Montell wouldn't listen. His arms were still tightly folded as he repeated his previous words even more loudly.

The man with the clipboard shook his head in despair. He walked over to a white car, got in and drove away.

Montell Collins grinned to himself and yelled after the car, "Don't bother coming back! I'm not moving!"

I hated to interrupt his gloating, but I had questions for him.

Putting a smile on my face, I approached him and said, "Hello. I don't know if you remember me—"

"From the café? Aye, I remember you. What are you doing here?"

"It's part of a follow-up service we offer." I'd already prepped Peggy on this lie I was using. "We'd like to ask you a few questions about the event at our café the other night. Have you got time to talk to us?"

"I've got all the time in the world. We'll talk on the doorstep if it's all the same to you. I want to keep an eye out for any more of those council numpties who might turn up. Think they can tell me to leave my home, they do. I keep telling them I'm going nowhere, and they can't make me!"

Peggy asked him, "Is yours a council house?"

"Mind your own business."

"If it is a council house, then don't the council have every right to ask you to leave?" she said.

Montell's eyes narrowed. "What's it got to do with you?"

"Nothing. I'm just saying. There's no harm in just saying something, is there? It's not against the law."

"Don't talk to me about the law!" Montell erupted. "I know all about the law, and how corrupt it is. And I don't need a know-it-all coming here and having a go at me about the law."

Peggy looked like she was going to launch into a full-blown argument. I didn't know how this conversation had escalated out of control so quickly.

I brought the conversation back to Theodosia and said to Montell, "We spoke briefly the other night. You were very pleased with the reading you had with Theodosia. Can you tell me more about it, please? If that's okay?"

He gave Peggy a swift glare before saying to me, "I had a great reading with her. As soon as she saw me, she knew I'd been born under a dark energy. She said I had an aura of despair around me which repelled other people, but that I was a magnet for bad luck. I'd been born under an unlucky star which I've always suspected. But I didn't know it was also in the wrong part of the sky when I came into this world."

Peggy said, "How can a star be in the wrong part of the sky? I've never heard such twaddle in all my life!"

Montell jabbed his finger at Peggy. "You're getting right on my nerves!"

"And you're getting on mine!" Peggy retaliated. "Karis, give me your car keys. I'll wait in the car for you. I can't stay here a second longer."

I handed the keys to her. She shot a filthy look at Montell before returning to the car.

"I'm sorry," I said to Montell. "I don't know what's got into her. She doesn't normally speak to people like that. Not until she's known them for a few minutes."

Montell broke into a good-natured smile. "It's okay. It's all part of my curse."

"Your curse?"

"Yeah. That's what Theodosia told me. Being born under that unlucky star cast a curse on me which explains a lot. I annoy people all the time. I have done all my life. Lots of people end up shouting at me. I don't mind. I like a good argument. Being under a curse explains a lot about my life. It explains why I bought a house on this street just before the council decided to knock them down. And it explains why I've been married six times. I keep getting the wrong women attaching themselves to me. It's got nothing to do with my personality, it's all the fault of that star-curse."

I didn't agree with his so-called curse but kept silent about it. "When you talked to me on the way out of the café, you said your luck was going to change. Why was that?"

"Theodosia removed my curse. She gave me a spiritual cleansing."

"Did she? How?"

"She lit a stick, waved it over me, and mumbled a magical chant. It was over in seconds. It must have started working straight away. I felt different. Invincible. I knew my luck had changed."

"And has it?"

He scratched his head. "I'm not sure yet. As soon as my reading was over, Theodosia asked me for two hundred and fifty pounds so she could buy some lottery tickets for me."

"She did?" I asked. "Why couldn't you buy them?"

"Because my new good luck was only temporary. That's what Theodosia said. My curse was so strong and she could only remove it for a short time, enough time for me to get home without any accidents. And I did get home safely. But I'd need a deeper spiritual cleanse to get rid of the curse once and for all. Theodosia said it could take a few appointments before it was gone completely."

"And how much was that going to cost?"

"Money doesn't matter when it comes to spiritual matters."

I asked, "What about those lottery tickets? What happened to those?"

Montell shrugged. "I don't know. Theodosia said she would let me know if I'd won anything. I haven't heard from her yet, so I'm assuming I didn't win."

He obviously didn't know Theodosia was dead. Should I tell him?

Montell made the decision for me. "Have you got another contact number for Theodosia? I've tried that one on her business card, and I've been trying to phone her all day to set up a cleansing appointment, but she's not returning my messages. I could do with another dose of good luck."

"I don't know how to say this. She's dead."

"Dead?"

"Yes."

"Dead?"

"Yes, dead."

"What do you mean?"

Why did people have trouble with that word?

"Dead. She's no longer alive. That kind of dead."

Montell put his hands in his pockets and rocked back and forth on his heels. "Dead, eh? That's annoying. What am I supposed to do about my spiritual cleaning out? I don't want all that bad luck coming back to me. Who's going to remove my star-curse now?"

"I don't know." I remembered how Theodosia had died. "Did you call on Theodosia at her house after your reading?"

"No. Why would I do that? Anyway, I don't know where she lives."

I frowned at him. "You just said you had her business card. Her address is on it."

"Is it? I didn't notice. Why are you asking if I went to her house?" Comprehension dawned on his face, swiftly followed by anger. "Did she die in her house? Was she murdered? Do you think I did it? That's why you're asking me, isn't it?"

It was the truth, but I was hardly going to admit that.

He asked, "Do you know how she died?"

"I do. The police came to see me. They said it was possibly during a break-in. They think she might have disturbed the thief."

He didn't say anything, but he gave me a studious look as if trying to read my mind to see if I had any more information.

I didn't say anything either. Sometimes, silence is more effective at getting people to talk.

In this case, it worked.

Montell looked left and right along the empty street. "I wouldn't be surprised if she was murdered. I thought Theodosia was a decent sort, and the advice she gave me was spot on, but I've heard other people weren't as happy with the advice she gave them."

"Which people?"

"I shouldn't say, but there was a young lass at your café the other night. She said she'd been to see Theodosia before, and had been given advice which she'd acted upon, but it hadn't turned out well for her. I asked her why she was back for another reading. She said she didn't have a choice. She was desperate."

I asked, "Do you know her name?"

"I do. I heard her talking to someone else that night, and she introduced herself. She's called Verity."

Verity. That was the young woman who was full of despair. The one who'd been feeling betrayed. I had her name and address on that file of Erin's.

I said, "Thank you for your help. And your feedback. What are you going to do about your house? Won't the council come back?"

"They will." He let out a big sigh. "Theodosia dying has ruined my plans for improving my luck. I'll get online and see if I can find anyone else who can help. There must be someone. Do you know of anyone?"

"I don't." I hesitated a little. "Are you sure she was telling you the truth about that star?"

"Of course I am. Why wouldn't she?"

"Okay, don't get angry, but I'm not convinced about her motivations for helping people. She could have told you that stuff about a cursed star just to get money from you. She already took two hundred and fifty pounds from you. And she was going to take more."

I let my words sink in.

Montell seemed to deflate in front of me. "You could be right about that. That would be just the thing that happens to me. Bad luck has followed me around all my life." He shook his head. "I might as well accept my fate."

"Or you could give yourself positive messages instead." I thought about the inspirational messages I'd seen online recently. "All change starts with the mind. You've got to believe it first, and then things will change. Something like that."

His face twisted in disgust. "You're mad. Just like that old woman in your car. I don't know why I attract folk like you two. Clear off!" He turned around, stormed into his house, and slammed his door.

I didn't mind because I had someone else to talk to.

Chapter 18

M y plan to visit Verity was postponed, because when I returned to my car I received a call from DI Fiona Knox.

"Ms Booth, I need to talk to you immediately. I'm five minutes away from your café. Can you meet me there?"

"I can. What is this about?"

"I'll tell you when I see you. What's your estimated time of arrival?"

"Erm, ten to fifteen minutes? Maybe twenty depending on the traffic."

Her sigh was audible. "Try and make it ten minutes." She ended the call.

I'd put the phone on loudspeaker so that Peggy could hear it.

Peggy's lips curled in disgust. "Rude woman. I wonder what she wants?"

"It must be something to do with the murder. I can't imagine it's a social call."

"She's probably come to her senses and realised she needs your help."

I pulled a face. "I doubt that. She doesn't know I'm psychic, and if she did, she wouldn't let me help. I know how she feels about people like me."

We set off for the café and arrived fifteen minutes later, which I thought was good considering the traffic around the new shopping centre. DI Knox was sitting at a corner table inside the café, her back as straight as a poker. Even though we'd made the journey in good time, when she saw us approaching she gave her watch a deliberate look whilst raising one eyebrow.

I almost felt like apologising for not getting there sooner, but then stopped myself. I had nothing to apologise for. I wasn't responsible for the traffic.

"Hello," I said as I approached her. I noticed the table was devoid of any cups or plates. "Would you like something to drink? Or eat?"

"No. I won't be staying. Who's this?" She directed a curt nod at Peggy.

"This is Peggy. My neighbour and good friend. Whatever you've got to say, you can say in front of Peggy." I sat down, so did Peggy. "Is this about Theodosia?"

DI Knox cast a suspicious glance at Peggy. "It is. I've been asked by DCI Parker to keep you informed of developments. Like I told you last time, I don't know why this is any of your concern. But DCI Parker thinks otherwise. I'm here to let you know we have arrested someone in connection with Theodosia Baker's death."

Peggy took a sharp intake of breath.

I said, "Oh? Are you able to tell us who that is?"

"I can." Her tone was reluctant. "It's a man by the name of Jed Humphreys."

"Jed Humphreys?" I repeated.

"Jed Humphreys?" Peggy echoed.

"Yes, Jed Humphreys." DI Knox scowled at us, which I thought was very rude. "He's a petty thief and is known at the station. Apparently."

"I don't understand," I said. "If he's a thief, then how is he responsible for Theodosia's death? Has he now turned to murder?"

"I don't know why you keep talking about murder. It's becoming an unhealthy obsession." Her scowl increased. She was going to end up with terrible wrinkles if she kept doing that. "Jed Humphreys recently committed thefts around the area where Ms Baker lived. He'd broken into homes and sheds in the homes adjacent to her house. Following calls from the homeowners of those properties, investigations were made and evidence taken. We matched fingerprints found on the scenes to those on our database. They belonged to Jed Humphreys. We subsequently found his fingerprints in Ms Baker's home." She checked her watch again.

"And?" I asked.

"And what?"

"Did he admit to killing her?"

"He denied it. He admitted to breaking into her house, but he claims she was already dead when he saw her. Despite seeing her lying dead on the ground, he proceeded to steal a few items before leaving her house." Her face was full of disgust. "He says he didn't take much as a mark of respect for the deceased."

My look of surprise matched Peggy's. For a moment, I didn't know what to say. But then I found my words. "Do you believe him?"

"That's none of your concern, Ms Booth. DCI Parker wanted you to be updated, and that's what I've done. You do not need to know anything else." She stood up.

"What about that notebook of Theodosia's?" I blurted out. I quickly realised I'd made a mistake.

"What notebook?" DI Knox asked.

I could hardly tell her I'd seen it in my vision. I quickly thought of a lie. "I saw her writing in a notebook when she was here. It had a list of names on one side, and a row of numbers at the other. It seemed very important to her. Did you find it at her home? Or was it stolen by Jed Humphreys?"

"I don't see that it's any of your business."

I couldn't help myself from saying, "It could be important. If Jed Humphreys didn't take it, then someone else did. Perhaps the person who murdered her. I only spoke to Theodosia for a few minutes, but I didn't like her. I imagine other people didn't either."

"I didn't like her at all!" Peggy announced. "She told me a load of lies about my late hubby. And she wanted to get money out of me. The charlatan!"

DI Knox looked at Peggy, and then back at me. She couldn't disguise the interest in her voice. "I'll make some enquiries about that notebook. It'll most likely be a waste of my time. But I'll check."

"And will you let us know?" I asked.

"I don't see why I should."

Peggy interjected, "But didn't Seb say you had to let us know about any developments?"

"He did, but I think I've told you more than enough." She gave us a disparaging look before walking away from us and out of the café.

Peggy tutted. "What an extremely rude woman."

"She's only doing her job, I suppose." I watched through the window as DI Knox got in her car and drove away. "I wonder if Jed Humphreys did kill Theodosia. And if it was because she disturbed him."

"I doubt it. You had a vision about her, and you clearly saw her being attacked." She took her phone from her handbag and tapped on it.

"Who are you phoning?"

"Seb, of course."

"Why?"

She put the phone to her ear. "To find out more about the case. Theodosia told me horrific lies about my Jeff. She must have done the same to others. And someone has got their revenge on her. I don't think that Jed bloke killed her. I can't stand by and let an innocent man go to jail. I just can't." She stopped talking. "Oh, heck. He's not answering. I'll leave him an urgent message."

Before I could stop her, Peggy left a message asking Seb to contact her as a matter of extreme urgency.

Chapter 19

Seb phoned her back within a few minutes. She put him on loudspeaker.

"Peggy? What's wrong? Is Karis okay?" Seb's words came out in a rush. "Is it the babies? Erin? Robbie? You?"

Peggy frowned at the phone. "Why am I last on your list? I'm insulted."

"Peggy! What's so urgent?"

"Okay. There's no need to shout. Everyone is fine. It's about the case."

"What case? What are you talking about? Is Karis there?"

"She is. She wants to know about the case too."

Seb took a deep breath. I imagined him silently counting to ten.

Peggy snapped, "Seb? Are you still there? Speak to me."

"I'm still here." His voice was considerably calmer. "I presume you're talking about Theodosia."

"Of course I am. Karis and I aren't dealing with any other cases at the moment. We can't do all your work for you."

"Can I speak to Karis? Please."

"If you must, but she's leaving the phone on loudspeaker, so just watch what you say. Don't get all soppy with her." She passed the phone to me.

"Hey there," I said. "How are you?"

"I'm fine." I smiled at the tenderness in his voice. "How are you?"

"He's fine too, by the sound of it," Peggy said. "What's happening with the case? That DI Knox has just spoken to us. Tell him what she said, Karis. Go on, tell him."

Under Peggy's watchful eye, I told Seb about DI Knox's short conversation with us. I finished with, "I didn't tell her about my vision concerning Theodosia's death. Seb, do you think I should tell her? I'd have to explain about my psychic abilities."

"I don't think that's wise. She's already reluctant to talk to you about the investigation, and I'm not sure I can ask her to give you any more information. She's doing me a huge favour by talking to you."

"I know. And I do appreciate it." I glanced at Peggy. I wanted to tell Seb about Jeff paying us a visit, but I'd have to make sure it was okay with Peggy first. I said to Seb, "I would like to know about the notebook, though. If it's with Jed Humphreys, then that's okay. But if it's not, that means someone else stole it."

"That would be the real murderer," Peggy said firmly. "They took that notebook because there's evidence in it which would implicate them. Implicate? Is that the right word?"

Seb said, "Let's not make presumptions. DI Knox will look at the facts and make a decision based on those." He paused. "Karis, is Peggy pulling a face at me?"

I smiled. "She is. Would you be able to find out about the notebook, and where it is? Just to put our minds at rest."

"I could try. But I'm in the middle of a class. I only excused myself because of the urgency of Peggy's message."

Peggy folded her arms and attempted to look innocent.

I felt a pang of guilt. "Seb, I don't want you to get into trouble."

"I won't. I know this is important to you. Can you give me a few hours? Once I'm finished with this class, I'll be free to contact Fiona."

"Who's Fiona?" Peggy asked.

"DI Knox," Seb and I replied at the same time.

"Humph. She doesn't look the type to have a first name," Peggy said.

Seb said, "I've got to go. I'll phone you later. Leave everything to Fiona until then. Okay?"

"Okay," I confirmed. Peggy looked away from me and didn't say anything.

As soon as I'd said goodbye to Seb, Peggy stood up and said, "Are you ready to go?"

"Go where?"

"To see Verity. Don't you need to do that fake follow-up thing with her? We need to find out what Theodosia said to her."

I almost said we should leave it to the police, but a niggling voice in my head told me we had to speak to Verity as soon as possible.

So, that's what we did.

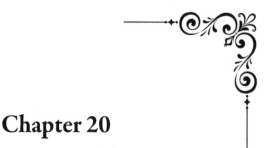

Chapter 20

When we first saw Verity Milligan, I thought I was looking at a ghost. We found her sitting on a bench in her back garden, pale and unmoving, her dark hair limp and lacklustre. She was staring into the distance.

"Is she dead?" Peggy whispered. "I didn't know you could die sitting up."

"She isn't dead," I replied quietly. "I don't think so, anyway."

I loudly cleared my throat as we walked towards the still figure. She blinked and looked at us.

"Hello!" I gave her a friendly wave. "Sorry to disturb you. We did knock at the front door, but there was no answer." I didn't add that Peggy had peeped through the front window before walking around the house and spotting Verity in the garden.

"Don't I know you?" Verity asked uncertainly. "You look familiar."

"I saw you recently at Erin's Café in town," I explained. "I own the café with my sister. You were there for a reading with Theodosia the other night."

She slowly nodded. "I remember now. What are you doing here?"

I went into the excuse about the follow-up service, which Verity readily accepted. I explained who Peggy was before asking if it was okay for us to take a seat.

She nodded before moving along the bench. Peggy and I sat down. I started with, "Have you heard the sad news about Theodosia?"

"I have." She resumed staring into space. "I saw something online."

I said, "You were very upset before your reading with Theodosia. Did you get the answers you were looking for?"

"I thought I did. But I was wrong. So very wrong. I don't want to talk about it."

Peggy's voice was full of kindness as she said, "I had a reading with Theodosia. She told me some terrible things, some awful lies. And, like a fool, I believed her. She turned my world upside down with her words. But I talked to Karis about it, and she made me see through the lies. It always helps to talk about things. Always."

Verity turned her head and looked at Peggy. A sad smile came to her face. "I feel such an idiot for believing Theodosia. I could feel in my heart that she was lying, but she was so convincing."

Peggy nodded. "I felt the same. She was an accomplished liar. She must have done it a lot over the years. Don't blame yourself. She took advantage of you. And me. No doubt, countless others too."

Verity said, "When I went to see her, I just had one question for her. I wanted to know if my husband, Andy, was cheating on me. We've only been married for six months, but all the signs were there. He'd work late, and he even worked over the weekends. He took phone calls in private and wouldn't say who was calling. My suspicious mind thought the worst."

I nodded as I recalled the feeling of betrayal I'd picked up on when I'd last seen Verity. "What did Theodosia say?"

"As soon as I asked my question, she said Andy was definitely cheating on me. And he had been since before we got married. She told me to leave him immediately. To close our joint accounts. See a solicitor. She gave me a lot of advice but I couldn't take it all in. I was in shock. Even though I suspected Andy of being unfaithful, I could not accept confirmation of it." She fell silent and looked at her lap.

"What happened after your reading?" I gently coaxed her.

Still looking down, she said, "Theodosia said I had to confront him. So I did. As soon as he got home, I accused him of cheating on me." She looked up. "Oh, the look in his eyes! Like I'd stabbed him in the heart. His face went all white. As soon as I'd said those accusing words, I knew I was wrong. And that Theodosia was wrong too. But I couldn't stop shouting at Andy. I couldn't control myself. He tried to explain himself, but I wouldn't listen. He grabbed his coat and left the house. He hasn't been back since."

"Have you phoned him?" I asked.

"Yes, hundreds of times. I've left messages saying I'm sorry, but he hasn't phoned me back. His best friend has been in touch with me. Andy is staying at his house. Andy is utterly devastated about what I said to him. And how I didn't trust him." Her voice cracked. "His friend told me Andy's been working late to earn extra money for the honeymoon we never had. Those secret phone calls were to confirm the travel details, and all the other treats Andy was planning to surprise me with on our honeymoon."

Peggy leaned over and patted Verity's hands. "You poor lass. But this can be fixed."

"It can't. I've tried."

"It can be fixed. I know it can," Peggy said firmly. "It might take time, but if you love each other as much as I think you do, then it will get sorted out. Love is a stubborn thing, it doesn't go away that easily. Did you tell Andy about your reading with Theodosia?"

"I did. That made him angry. He asked why I was telling a stranger about our problems."

Peggy said, "I'd be more than happy to talk to your husband. I can tell him how manipulative Theodosia was, and how I fell for her act too. That might help."

"You'd do that?"

Peggy nodded. "I would. Do you have an address for him?"

"I do." Verity gave us an address which Peggy tapped into her phone.

I asked, "Did Theodosia give you her business card after the reading?"

"She did. She said she offers counselling services, and that I might need them after my marriage break up. She said she'd give me a discount on her rates."

I heard a quiet curse coming from Peggy.

A flicker of hope alighted in Verity's eyes. "Do you think there's a chance Andy will forgive me? After what I've done?"

Peggy replied, "Of course. I'll make him see sense. Do you know if he'll be at that address now?"

"He will. He's taken a few days off work, according to his friend." Her eyes brimmed with tears. "He's too upset to do anything but lie in bed. It's all my fault."

"No, it isn't," I said. "It's Theodosia's fault. Please, don't blame yourself."

Peggy stood up. "We'll go and see him now. The sooner this mess is sorted out, the better. You take care of yourself. Wipe your tears away. Your husband will be back in your arms soon. You'll see." She moved over to Verity and hugged her.

I did the same and then headed back to the car with Peggy. As we drove away, I said, "This is a kind thing you're doing."

"Maybe. But I have an ulterior motive."

I sighed. "You don't even have to tell me what that is. You think Andy is a murder suspect. Am I right?"

"You are." She shook her head sadly. "I really hope he isn't the murderer. That young woman will be devastated if he is."

Chapter 21

"Is he dead?" Peggy asked me.

We were looking at Andy Milligan as he lay on the sofa staring at the ceiling. His friend had let us into his house without hesitation and told us to, 'Sort him out.' He had then promptly left us alone with the pale-faced man.

"Hello," I began politely. "I'm Karis, and this is Peggy. We'd like to have a word with you, please. It's about Verity. Your wife." The last part was unnecessary but I couldn't help it.

Andy's face crumpled like a tissue. He turned away from us and buried his head in the sofa.

I tried again. "Sorry to intrude, but we'd like to talk to you. It won't take long."

Muffled sobs came from the young man.

Peggy muttered something about bad manners and marched over to Andy. She tapped him roughly on the shoulder. "Turn around and talk to us. We haven't got all day." She moved closer to his one exposed ear. "Turn around. Now!"

Andy yelped, and then turned around to face us. His cheeks were wet with tears. "I don't know who you are but I'm not talking about Verity. I'm trying to forget her."

"Tough," Peggy said. "Sit up. I'm not having this conversation with you lying there like a sloth." Andy swiftly sat up. Peggy flapped her hands at him. "Shift up. There are three of us who need to fit on this sofa."

I felt a pang of sympathy for Andy who had been happily wallowing in self-pity a few minutes ago. Happily? Maybe not.

Peggy sat next to Andy, and I sat next to Peggy. I wasn't sure who was going to speak to Andy first. Thankfully, Peggy took immediate control.

"Now then, young man," she began in her no-nonsense voice, "we're going to talk about that lovely wife of yours."

"I don't want to talk about—"

"I don't care what you want," Peggy interrupted him. "I'm talking. You're listening. Your wife had the misfortune of recently talking to a person of an unscrupulous nature."

"Eh?" Andy said.

"Your wife went for a psychic reading the other day. She told you that. The psychic was an evil woman who told Verity a pack of malicious lies about you. The psychic also told me a load of lies about my late husband. She was extremely persuasive. She fooled me. She fooled your wife too. We've just spoken to Verity, and as soon as she'd accused you of cheating, she knew in her heart that it wasn't true."

"I did try to tell her that," Andy pointed out. "But she wouldn't stop shouting at me. I've never seen her like that before."

"She was under the influence of that evil creature," Peggy explained. "She got into Verity's head, like she did mine. Verity is genuinely sorry about what she said to you. She thinks you're never going to forgive her. She's devastated that you've left her."

"Is she? I thought she'd be glad to see the back of me, considering what she accused me of."

"She's beside herself with grief. And so are you. You've both been victims of a scam. That psychic was intending to make money from Verity."

Andy sat up straighter. "She was? She was going to do that to my wife? What's the name of this psychic?"

"It doesn't matter now. She's dead." Peggy let the words sink in.

"Dead? Properly dead?"

Peggy frowned. "What other kind of dead is there? She died in dubious circumstances of a suspicious nature."

"Eh?"

"She was murdered. That's what I think, anyway." Peggy gave him a penetrating look as if trying to get into his brain. "Did you kill her?"

Andy's eyebrows shot up so quickly that I thought they were going to fly right off his head. "No! I didn't even know her name. You'll be asking me next if I've got an alibi for when she died. Stop looking at me like that!"

"Have you got an alibi?" Peggy's piercing stare was starting to unnerve me too.

He nervously ran his hand through his hair. "When did she die? I've been here since that argument with Verity days ago. I haven't even left the house."

Peggy quizzed him about what time he left his marital home, how long it took him to arrive at this house, and if his friend could confirm that.

Once she was satisfied Andy wasn't the murderer, she patted him good-naturedly on the knee. "Thanks for that information. We'll be on our way now. I suggest you go and see your wife immediately. You need to talk." She sniffed. "Have a shower first. We'll see ourselves out. Come on, Karis."

Like a queen taking leave of her subjects, Peggy rose smoothly from the sofa and headed towards the door. I thanked Andy for his time before following her in a less regal manner.

We were stopped from leaving by Andy calling out, "I don't think Verity will want to see me. Not after all she said. I just know she won't."

Peggy sighed. "Of course she will. Phone her now. Explain you've spoken to us. I told her we were coming here to see you."

He twisted his hands together. "I can't."

"Give me your phone and I'll do it." Peggy put her hand out.

Andy stood up and came over to us. He gave his phone to Peggy who immediately began to scroll through it. I saw her eyes widen. I looked over her shoulder at the name which had caught her attention.

Lying a little, I said to Andy, "Jed Humphreys? I think I know someone of that name. Is he a friend of yours?"

"Sort of. He's Verity's uncle. Her dad's brother. I'm not sure what his job is, but he always gives us expensive presents for birthdays and Christmas. And he insisted on paying for most of our wedding. Verity's dad passed away when she was ten. Jed has been more like a father to her than an uncle. He'd do anything for Verity. Anything."

Chapter 22

Before Peggy and I could question Andy further about Jed Humphreys, I got yet another phone call from DI Knox which lasted five seconds. She was livid and told us to get down to the police station immediately.

Peggy did make a quick call to Verity before leaving Andy. As soon as Verity answered, Peggy shoved the phone in Andy's face and said, "Talk to your wife."

Not long after, we arrived at the police station. We announced our presence to the police officer on reception and were told to take a seat. Peggy refused to sit down and stood near the door. She said she wanted to make a quick getaway if things turned nasty.

"Why would they turn nasty?" I asked her.

"You heard the tone in the inspector's voice. Like she was spitting feathers. You've obviously done something to upset her. I'm innocent in all this. I don't want to be part of your investigation, Karis. There's no need for me to be on the sharp end of the inspector's tongue. Not at my advanced years. I can't be doing with that kind of stress. I'm delicate. And fragile."

I pursed my lips. "You're as delicate and fragile as a lump of steel. Go home, if you want to. I'll deal with DI Knox on my own."

Peggy cast a wistful look at the doors. Then she came over to me and sat down. "I won't leave you to deal with the dragon on your own."

"Dragon? What dragon?" DI Knox appeared seemingly out of nowhere. She was holding an electronic tablet in one hand. Her face was devoid of any emotion, even her eyes were blank. She reminded me of a life-sized robot I'd once seen at a futuristic event at an art gallery.

Peggy grabbed my elbow. "Crikey! You scared the living daylights out of me! Where did you come from?"

DI Knox ignored Peggy's question. She glanced at her tablet, swiped her finger across it, and then spoke to me in icy tones. "We spoke about Jed Humphreys earlier. Do you recall that conversation?"

"Yes." Her piercing stare was much more severe than Peggy's earlier one.

"Jed Humphreys is about to be interviewed." She stopped speaking. Her nostrils flared. It looked like she was holding onto her patience by the thinnest of threads. "DCI Parker has requested you be allowed to watch the interview."

"Both of us?" Peggy asked. "It should be both of us."

What happened to her not wanting to be part of the investigation?

DI Knox answered, "Yes, both of you. For the record, I am against this. I do not like civilians interfering with my investigations. But it appears DCI Parker has some friends in high places. I suspect strings have been pulled. Peculiar handshakes have been exchanged too, no doubt. Come with me. Don't say a word."

We followed DI Knox through a series of doors until we came to a darkly lit corridor.

She pointed to the carpet. "Stand there. Don't move. Don't speak. Stay right there until I come back. Do you understand me?"

We nodded silently like chastised children.

She opened a door in front of us which I hadn't even noticed in the darkness. She went through it and closed it firmly behind her. All of a sudden, a room in front of us was illuminated.

Peggy whispered excitedly, "It's one of those interview rooms! I've seen them on the TV. We must be behind a two-way mirror thing." She let out a noise which sounded suspiciously like a giggle.

I put my finger to my lips and nodded at the glass which was separating us from the room.

"Oh, right. Yes," Peggy whispered. "They might be able to hear us. They can't on the TV, though. Ooo, look! The other door's opening now. The prisoner must be coming in."

Jed Humphreys entered the room. I couldn't help but feel disappointed. I was expecting a spry, shifty-looking man who knew his way around a five-lever mortise lock. Or a stocky bloke with the wisdom of a thousand years in his eyes. But Jed Humphreys was a normal-looking man. Mousy brown hair. Eyes the colour of mud. Dull complexion. Medium build. He didn't even have any scars or a pronounced limp.

I shared a look with Peggy. She looked as disappointed as me. She whispered, "I was expecting a lot more."

"Me too. At least one scar."

Peggy's face lit up. "Just a minute. Oh, that's clever. He's made himself look boring on purpose. When any witnesses try to describe him after he's committed a crime, they won't be able to list any distinguishing marks. He's a genius."

It was soon clear Jed Humphreys was not a genius. When questioned by DI Knox, he openly admitted to breaking into many premises along the street where Theodosia had lived. He even pointed out the ones DI Knox had missed in nearby streets. He said he had no knowledge of any notebook in Theodosia's house, and asked why would he steal a notebook anyway.

When DI Knox asked him about Theodosia, Jed began to fidget in his seat. Sweat broke out on his forehead. His voice rose as he declared over and over again that he had nothing to do with her death. Despite his protests, DI Knox calmly repeated her questions about Theodosia. Maybe she was hoping to catch Jed out in a lie.

As Jed's protests became louder, I felt a familiar tingle. I signalled to Peggy I was getting a vision. She put her hand on my back in an attempt to steady me should I fall over. I hoped I wouldn't fall over because I'd easily squash her.

The vision came to me quickly and only lasted a few seconds. When it was over, I said to Peggy, "I saw Jed breaking into Theodosia's house. He did get in via the unlocked bathroom window, just like he said. He looked at a list of addresses on a piece of paper. Theodosia's name was the last one on the list. There was a figure of two thousand pounds written next to it. Perhaps he was paid to break into her house. And maybe those other houses too."

"Why would someone pay him to do that?"

"To make it look like he was the murderer. He's left his fingerprints all over her house. And the other houses he broke into. If he's an experienced thief, why wasn't he wearing gloves?"

"And why would he implicate himself in a murder by leaving fingerprints? Two thousand pounds doesn't seem enough money to make him do that."

"If the murderer paid him to break into Theodosia's house, which it looks that way, maybe they were also bribing Jed with something to make sure he did go ahead with the thefts." I frowned. "But then why pay him any money at all?"

"That is strange."

I said, "I could feel how scared Jed was. How apprehensive. As if he were expecting something bad to happen."

"Like finding a body?"

"Maybe."

DI Knox's interview with Jed abruptly ended. He was led away. A few seconds later, the stern-faced inspector was in front of us. I decided it was time to tell her the truth about my psychic ability and the visions I'd had.

But I never got the chance.

DI Knox opened a door behind us, another one which I hadn't noticed, and it made me wonder if the police station was full of secret doors. With barely controlled anger, she said, "Out. Now. No matter what strings DCI Parker continues to pull, we will have no further contact. I will see to that. If you so much as phone me, I will have you arrested for wasting police time. The exit is down that corridor behind you."

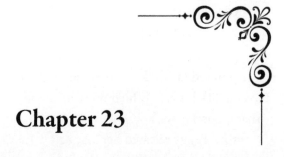

Chapter 23

Peggy and I left the police station quickly before DI Knox decided to have us escorted out.

Peggy complained about how much she disliked DI Knox, and how we should make a formal complaint about her lack of manners and brusque manner.

I nodded vaguely. Somewhere in my brain, a nugget of important information was trying to make itself known. Montell Collins had said something about someone, and it was important. But like a slippery fish, my mind could not latch on to the information.

It was only when we were driving away that I remembered what it was.

"Verity had a previous reading with Theodosia!" I declared.

"Did she? Hang on, how do you know?"

"Montell told me. I've only just remembered. We never asked Verity about that when we spoke to her." I shot a look at Peggy. "We should visit her again on the pretence of checking up on her. We could see if she's sorted things out with her husband."

Peggy said, "That's an excellent idea. I genuinely do want to know what's happened between her and her hubby. I hope they've patched things up. I don't suppose there's any harm in talking about Theodosia again whilst we're there."

I casually added, "And we can ask her about her Uncle Jed too. I wonder if she knows he's been arrested."

"If she doesn't, I'm not going to be the one who tells her."

"Me neither."

We soon pulled up outside Verity's house. We noticed a red car in the driveway which hadn't been there earlier.

I pointed at it. "I saw that car at the house Andy was staying at. I assume it's his car. Which must mean he's returned home." I smiled. "That is good news."

"It is." Peggy released her seat belt. "They're probably having some private time together. Let's say hello."

"Shouldn't we leave them alone?"

"No. They'll be glad to see us. They'll want to thank us for our help. I hope they offer us a cup of tea. I haven't had a drink for hours. My throat's parched."

She got out of the car and walked up to the front door. I stayed where I was and waited. Peggy knocked on the door. It remained closed. She knocked twice more, her knocks getting louder each time. When the door didn't open, she turned her puzzled face to me. I pointed to the upstairs window. Peggy glanced upwards, noticed the closed curtains, and swiftly returned to the car.

She got in, fastened her seat belt, and said, "We'll come back when they've finished making up. Where are we going now?"

"I want to have another word with Montell. I want to know if Verity said anything else to him about her previous visit to Theodosia. I also want to know more about how people booked their appointments at the café with Theodosia. Montell said something about getting an email invitation. Before we go there, we can pop into a café on the way. I could do with a cup of tea too."

Peggy gave me directions to a cosy café which she'd been to before. It wasn't that far away. Once inside the café, we decided to take advantage of the delicious homemade cakes which were on display.

Thirty minutes later, we left the place feeling satisfyingly full. It didn't take us long to reach Paradise Road.

Peggy said, "Park a few houses away from Montell's. I'm staying in the car again. I don't want to be anywhere near him. There's something about that man which rattles my cage."

"It'll be the cursed star he was born under," I said in a serious tone. "He can't help it."

"Pah! His personality has nothing to do with a curse. He's just plain annoying." She sighed. "If you really need my help when you start talking to him, just give me a wave and I'll join you."

"I will."

As we turned into Paradise Road, I almost collided with a silver car which was coming the other way. I swerved just in time, throwing poor Peggy to one side.

"Are you all right?" I asked.

"I am. No thanks to the idiot who was driving that car! They were almost on our side of the road. Did they even see you?"

"No. But I saw the driver. It was Bonita Stevens."

"Who?"

"She's the woman who had the first reading with Theodosia. The one who declared her love for a colleague in front of everyone. What's she doing here?"

"She must have been visiting Montell Collins. There's no one else who lives on this street," Peggy pointed out.

I stopped the car. "Do we talk to Montell as planned? Or go after Bonita and see where she's going? And why she was on this street?"

Chapter 24

I turned the car around and followed Bonita. She drove towards the new shopping centre and got lost in the traffic for a while, but I managed to locate her ahead of us.

"Excellent tailing," Peggy said.

"Thanks." I was feeling quite smug with myself.

My smug feeling vanished as soon as we got near the car park. Lines of cars were queued up, all waiting to get into the precious few spaces which were left. I slowed down as I joined the end of the queue.

Peggy tutted. "What's all the fuss about? It's only a shopping centre. The whole world and his dog have turned up. Where did Bonita go? Can you see her anywhere?"

I craned my neck. "She's five cars ahead. Just a minute, we're moving. Keep your eyes on her."

We moved all of three inches.

"Look!" Peggy pointed. "She just nipped into that space. Did you see how quickly she drove into it? Very nifty. Can you park near her?"

"Not at the moment." I scanned the area. "I can't see any spaces at all. We could be here for ages."

"She's getting out. We're going to lose her." Peggy reached for the door handle. "I'm going after her. We can't let her get away."

"We can. I know where she lives. We don't have to talk to her here."

The sparkle of glee in Peggy's eyes almost blinded me. "But this is more exciting. I've always wanted to follow someone through a busy shopping centre. We'll keep in radio contact."

"Radio contact?"

"I mean our phones. I'll keep you informed of my whereabouts. I won't let you down." She left the car, ducked her head, and scuttled after Bonita. She couldn't have looked more conspicuous if she'd tried.

It took me twenty minutes of inching slowly forward before I found a parking space. It was at the very far end of the car park. I hadn't kept 'radio contact' with Peggy because I couldn't use my phone when driving, even though I was driving at a snail's pace.

As soon as I parked up, I took my phone from my handbag and saw I had twenty voice messages.

I listened to them as I got out of the car. They were all from Peggy. They detailed her journey through the shopping centre as she covertly followed Bonita. Not only did she point out where Bonita was, Peggy informed me about the shops which were inside the new centre, what they were selling, and some of the supposed discounts they were offering. Peggy didn't think much of the shops or their prices.

I caught up with Peggy in the clothes department of a larger shop. She was whispering something into her phone and hadn't seen me approaching.

I tapped her lightly on her shoulder. She shoved her phone in her pocket. "Nothing! I'm doing nothing. I'm not talking to anyone!" Her features relaxed. "Oh, Karis, it's you. You took your time."

"I know. It's crazy out there. Where's Bonita?"

"She's in the changing rooms. Trying on a navy dress which has a white collar. It's not going to do anything for her skin tone. She should have gone for another colour. They've got the dress in a lovely shade of purple." Peggy stiffened. "Shh. She's coming back out. I've done a grand job of following her. I've been like a shadow. But a shadow you can't see."

I frowned. "How would I know the shadow is there if I can't see it?"

Peggy's eyes widened. She hissed, "She's coming closer."

Bonita walked straight up to us. She looked at Peggy and said, "Why are you following me?"

"I am not following you!" Peggy said. "How dare you accuse me of such a thing?"

Bonita turned my way. "You too? Has this got something to do with Theodosia?"

"Yes." I decided the truth was better than trying to deny Peggy's actions. "We saw you leaving Paradise Road earlier."

"You almost crashed into us," Peggy accused her.

"Did I? When was this?"

"About forty minutes ago," I said. "Paradise Road is where Montell Collins lives. He was at Theodosia's reading too."

Bonita nodded. "Yes, I know. I talked to him the other night. Or rather, I listened whilst he shouted at me."

"Why did he shout at you?" I asked.

"He was expecting some paperwork from me. I'd forgotten all about it because my mind had been on other things, as you know, but Montell loudly reminded me of it the other night. He worked in the sales department at my office for a few weeks. It was months ago. He was useless. I'm surprised he even lasted a few weeks. He annoyed everyone he spoke to. Staff and customers. I was supposed to send some papers to confirm his time with us, and all the other documents which were needed. I'd forgotten to do it. I apologised and said I'd post the paperwork. He said that wasn't good enough and he wanted it hand-delivered the next day."

"Bloomin' cheek," Peggy said.

"I know," Bonita agreed. "I put the papers in my handbag the next day. Then I had that awful situation with Raff. I left the office in a rush and forgot all about Montell. I only remembered the papers after you left my house earlier. Talking to you made me want to put the horrible business with Raff in the past. I made a list of things to do, and that's when I remembered the paperwork. I thought I might as well deliver it as soon as possible. I had his address, and I put the papers through his letterbox. I didn't want to talk to him. He makes me angry for some reason."

Peggy nodded in understanding.

Bonita carried on, "I thought I might pop in here to see what all the fuss is about. I wish I hadn't now. It's packed. And I don't think much of the extortionate prices."

"Me neither," Peggy said. In a swift change of subject, she asked, "I don't suppose you know anyone called Jed Humphreys."

"No, I don't think so. His name doesn't sound familiar. Who is he?"

"Nobody," I said. I didn't want to get into an explanation about him being arrested for Theodosia's murder. I recalled how evasive she'd looked earlier when I'd asked her about calling on Theodosia after her reading. I asked her the same question now.

She looked away from us. "You've already asked me that."

"I know. And you lied to me." I was taking a chance. I didn't know if she'd been lying or not.

Bonita looked back at us. "Okay. I did lie. I did go to Theodosia's house. I complained about the advice she'd given me. She said her advice had been correct, but that I'd gone about declaring my love in the wrong way. According to her, I shouldn't have done it in front of so many people. She said I'd frightened Raff off. Then she told me he still loved me, and wanted me to declare my love again but only when we were alone. Do you know what she did then?"

"No. What?" Peggy asked.

With a voice full of bitterness, Bonita said, "She held her hand out and asked for money! She said fifty pounds should cover the advice she'd just given me. I couldn't believe the nerve of her. I knew then what sort of a person she was. I was furious with myself for going to see her. And I was furious with her too."

Her cheeks flushed with anger. It was on the tip of my tongue to ask her if she'd killed Theodosia.

Peggy beat me to it. "Did you kill her?"

"What? No! Of course I didn't!" She put a hand on her chest and backed up. "I can't believe you've asked me that. How dare you! I'm leaving now. Don't follow me. If you do, I'll call the police."

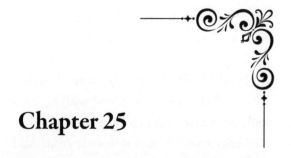

Chapter 25

We left the shopping centre and returned to Verity's house hoping that she'd be able to see us now.

Neither I nor Peggy were convinced Bonita Stevens was completely innocent. I felt like she was hiding something from us, but that could have been my suspicious mind going into overdrive.

As we walked along the path to Verity's front door, we heard laughter coming from the garden. We followed the noise and found Verity and Andy sitting on the bench. They were holding hands and gazing into each other's eyes with soft smiles on their faces. It was an intimate moment and I hated to interrupt them. But I did it anyway.

"Hi!" I called out. "Sorry to disturb you." I wasn't sorry at all, but it was the polite thing to say.

Verity blushed. "Hello. You're not disturbing us. I'm glad you're here. Thank you so much for explaining everything to Andy."

Peggy said, "It looks like you've made up."

Verity blushed some more. "We have. Would you like a cup of tea? Or a coffee?"

I shared a look with Peggy. I hardly ever said no to a cup of tea, and Peggy didn't either, but I felt like we were in the way. It was obvious the couple wanted to be alone. "No, thank you. Can we have a chat with you? It won't take long."

Andy said, "I'll get some chairs for you. Just a minute." He kissed Verity's hand before racing to the other side of the garden to grab a couple of wooden chairs. He was back at our side in a flash with them.

He returned to Verity and took her hand in his. They resumed their love-struck gazes at each other. I felt like a total gooseberry.

Peggy and I took a seat. No one spoke for a moment or two.

I said, "Verity, I hate to bring up the subject of Theodosia again, but I was told the reading you had with her wasn't the first one, and that you'd been to see her before. Is that right?"

Verity tore her attention away from Andy. "What? Who told you that?"

"A man called Montell Collins. He was at the café event too. He said you'd told him about a previous reading you'd had with Theodosia. Do you remember speaking to him?"

She frowned. "I did have a strange conversation with an older man. He kept moaning about his bad luck, and how he was born under an unlucky something or other. Is that the same man?"

I nodded. "What was your conversation about?"

"It was weird. After we went upstairs at the café, Theodosia called out to us from behind her curtain. She told us to sit on the floor and meditate on what we wanted from the reading. We had to wait until our names were called. That older man sat next to me. We were supposed to close our eyes, but he was giving me a weird look like he'd seen me somewhere before but couldn't remember where from."

"Did you recognise him from anywhere?"

"No. I closed my eyes and tried to ignore him, but I could still feel him staring. Then he suddenly said, 'Jed! Jed Humphreys!' That's my uncle's name. I opened my eyes and asked if he knew Jed. He did. He said he'd recognised me from some wedding photographs which Uncle Jed had on his walls."

I asked, "Where does your uncle live?"

"Just a few streets away from here. But he used to live on Paradise Road. But those houses are being pulled down now. That man at the reading, Montell was it?"

I nodded.

"Montell said he'd been to Uncle Jed's house on Paradise Road and seen his photos." Verity smiled. "Uncle Jed has a lot of photos of me. He's more like a dad than an uncle. He's even kept terrible drawings I did as a child. He had some of them framed as if they were works of art."

I asked, "Did Montell say if he was a neighbour of your uncle's? He lives on Paradise Road too."

"He didn't say. We didn't talk after that. I certainly didn't tell him I'd had a previous reading with Theodosia because I hadn't had one. He must have got me mixed up with someone else."

Peggy spoke, "Something's been bothering me about the event the other night. Well, lots of things are bothering me. But the main one is, how did you know about the event? As far as Karis and I know, it wasn't publicised." She looked at me. "Or was it? We didn't have any posters in the window. Or anything online. Did we?"

I shook my head. "Maybe Erin intended to do that, but in her exhausted state, she completely forgot. Verity, how did you find out about it?"

Verity looked at Andy. "I'm so sorry about what I'm going to say next. I did something awful. Please, don't judge me."

He tucked a stray wisp of hair behind her ear. "I won't judge you. What was done is history. All that matters now is our future."

She gave him an uncertain look. "You might not think that in a minute. Andy, when you started working late, and then having those private phone calls, my mind went to dark places. Like an idiot, I went online and looked for signs of people having affairs. I went on social media and asked for help there too." Her eyes filled with tears. "I'm so sorry for doubting you."

He shook his head. "It's my fault. I'm sorry for not telling you why I was working extra hours. Don't blame yourself."

Bringing the conversation back to the deceased psychic, I asked, "What has this got to do with Theodosia?"

Verity explained, "Not long after I started discussing my fears on social media, I kept seeing ads for Theodosia. They were very eye-catching and mentioned things like marital problems, suspicions about your partner, and that kind of thing. It felt like the ads were speaking to me personally. I was desperate at the time, so I clicked on the ads. I was taken to Theodosia's website and given an offer for a free reading on the phone. I only spoke to Theodosia for a few minutes, but she was very sympathetic and helpful. She said she needed to see me in person. She took my email and a few weeks later I got an invite to her event at your café."

"That's interesting," Peggy said. "It's almost like she targeted her ads at you."

I was thinking the same thing. "Verity, you said your uncle lived on Paradise Road. What number did he live at?"

"Number forty-eight."

I tried to control my shock. That was where Montell lived. What was the connection between him and Jed?

I couldn't think of any more questions for Verity. And I wanted to talk to Montell Collins as soon as possible.

Standing up, I said, "Thanks for talking to us. We'll leave you in peace."

Verity said to Andy, "I haven't heard from Uncle Jed in a few days. Have you?"

"No. I'm sure he'll be in touch soon. You know he can't go long without checking on you to see if you're okay."

"I hope so." Verity's brow creased. "I can't help but worry about him. I hope he's not in any trouble."

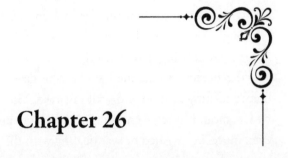

Chapter 26

"What are we doing back here?" Peggy asked me a short while later. "This is the last place we should be."

"I know, but there's something I have to do." I turned the car engine off and stared at the building in front of us. "I'll deal with the consequences. And there will be consequences."

"But why now? I thought we were going to see Montell."

"We were. But I've got an overwhelming urge to be here. I have to talk to her. Tell her everything. And then wait for the insults."

"And possibly a jail sentence!" Peggy said. "You heard her threats earlier. She said she'd arrest us if she saw us again."

"I know. You stay here. I'll talk to her on my own."

"No chance. We're in this together."

I gave her a grateful smile. "Thanks. You'll have to let me do all the talking."

"I'll try my best, but if she starts having a go at you, she'll have me to deal with."

I opened the door. "Come on, before I lose my courage."

We went into the police station and asked for DI Knox. I was half hoping she wouldn't be in, but alas, she was.

When the detective appeared in front of us, her look was as stony as a museum full of statues. She didn't say a word as she loomed over us suddenly seeming two feet taller.

"I need to talk to you," I began. "It's important. Very important. It concerns Theodosia and her death. When I've finished talking, you can throw me out of the station. Or lock me up for wasting police time. Although, I don't think I am wasting your time." I pointed to Peggy. "Peggy has nothing to do with this. Don't take your anger out on her."

The detective remained silent. She gave us the slightest of nods before turning around and walking away. She took us into Seb's office which should have given me more courage, but it made me miss him even more. I so wished he was dealing with this case.

But he wasn't.

DI Knox was.

The inspector closed the door, indicated for us to sit, and then sat behind the desk in Seb's chair.

Despite my nerves, I proceeded to tell her about my psychic ability. I gave her a few details about previous murders which I'd witnessed in my visions, and how I'd told Seb about them. I added that Seb and I had known each other since childhood and he'd known about my abilities since then. I kept expecting DI Knox to make a disparaging comment, or to throw us out. But, unnervingly, she did neither. She just looked at me without saying a word.

I carried on regardless. I told her about my recent visions concerning Theodosia. Her silence started to annoy me. She could have the decency to at least acknowledge my words! My anger caused me to tell her about the investigations I'd been making, and how I thought the police should have been making those enquiries and not me.

When I'd finished speaking, I stood up and said, "I've got a strong feeling that Montell Collins has something to do with Theodosia's murder. And I do know she was murdered, it wasn't an accident. I'm going to talk to him now. Would you like me to tell you what he says?"

She finally spoke. "No." She stood up. "I'm coming with you."

Relief washed through me. I smiled. "You believe me? About my visions?"

Her laugh was harsh. "Of course not! You're a deluded fool. And so is DCI Parker for believing you. I'll make sure his superiors hear about his association with you. I'm going with you to see Montell Collins. I'm going to be right at your side when you accuse him of murder. And then when he complains about you, which he will do, I'm going to arrest you in front of him." She looked at Peggy. "You can go home. In view of your age, I'll try to forget you had anything to do with this nonsense."

Peggy's eyes narrowed. "I don't need your pity. I'm going with Karis. I want to be there when you apologise to her. You'll soon realise she's been telling you the truth. And I want to see the look on your smug face when that happens."

"Fine," DI Knox retorted in an unprofessional manner.

"Fine!" Peggy added.

I sighed. I was not looking forward to what was going to happen next. Not just the confrontation between Montell and me, but the subsequent argument between Peggy and DI Knox. Someone was going to be proved right.

I just hoped it was me.

Chapter 27

"About time too!" Montell Collins proclaimed when he looked at DI Knox's identification.

"About time?" she repeated.

"Yes. You are here about my house, aren't you? I've complained to your lot endlessly for the last few weeks. It's about time you had the decency to take my complaints seriously."

"I'm not following," the inspector said.

"My complaints about the council. And how they can't knock my house down. That's why you're here isn't it?" He stopped talking when he noticed Peggy and me half hiding behind the inspector's back. "Hang on, what are those two doing here? Have they complained about me? I bet they have, especially the old one. She looks the complaining type. What's she been saying about me?"

"Mr Collins, I am not here about some council matter. May I come in? I do not care to discuss police business on the street."

Montell paled. "Police business? What kind of police business?"

"You'll find out when you let us in," DI Knox said sternly. She took a step forward.

Montell barred her way. He cast a nervous glance over his shoulder into his house. "Can't we talk at the police station?"

"No. I want to talk to you now. Is there a problem with that?"

Sweat broke out on his forehead indicating that there was indeed a problem.

DI Knox spotted his discomfort too. She strode over the threshold causing him to move to one side.

"It's not what you think!" Montell cried out as he rushed after the inspector.

Peggy and I weren't far behind. We found DI Knox in the living room looking at a large amount of money strewn across a table. Montell was at her side sweating profusely.

Peggy let out a gasp. "Blimey! Have you robbed a bank? Where did all that money come from?"

"I...I..." Montell swallowed nervously. "I can explain."

"I would like that very much," DI Knox informed him. "How much money is on your table?"

He swallowed again. "About ten thousand pounds. I haven't finished counting it yet."

DI Knox gave him a slow nod. "And where did this money come from?"

He pulled at the top of his T-shirt as if hoping to get some air on to his reddening neck and chest. "From here and there. Money I've made from odd jobs I've done over the years. I don't trust banks. I normally keep my money under my mattress. Thought I'd get it out and count it. Yeah, that's what I'm doing. Counting my money. *My* money. That's not illegal, is it."

DI Knox didn't say anything. She had a look on her face which Seb gets sometimes when he's talking to Peggy, the look when he's trying to find his patience.

I was interested to hear what the inspector was going to say next. As I moved a step closer, a sudden vision flashed into my head. It lasted a few seconds.

I turned away from the compelling sight in front of me and headed towards the kitchen. I stopped at the doorway and looked at the third cupboard along. There was a square biscuit tin on the top of it, just like I'd seen in my vision. I was tempted to take the tin down and look inside but realised that would be a stupid thing to do.

"DI Knox!" I called out. "Can you come here, please? Urgently."

I thought she was going to ignore me, but thankfully, she didn't. I heard her ordering Montell not to move a muscle, and then telling Peggy to make sure he didn't.

"What is it?" she snapped as she approached me. "Can't you see I'm busy?"

I pointed to the biscuit tin. "Whether you believe my visions or not, I've had one concerning that biscuit tin. I haven't touched it. And I haven't stepped a foot into the kitchen."

"Biscuit tin? This is not the time for snacking!"

"You need to look inside the tin. Now. Please."

She hesitated a second, and then moved forward. She put latex gloves on before reaching for the tin. She came closer to me before opening it. She looked at the contents. Her eyebrows rose. "Is this...?"

"Theodosia's notebook? Yes, it is. Montell took it. Which only means one thing."

"I know what it means, Ms Booth. I'm not stupid. Follow me."

We returned to the living room. Montell was perspiring badly now. Peggy, at a foot smaller than him, had her arms stretched out as if getting ready to stop him from making his escape.

DI Knox held the notebook up. "Mr Collins, I think you've got some explaining to do."

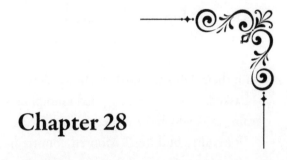

Chapter 28

Montell staggered over to the sofa and collapsed into it. "I didn't mean for it to go that far. I didn't mean to kill her. I was just going to talk to her, but then I saw her smirking face when she opened the door. Anger went right through me, like one of those tidal wave things. I couldn't help myself."

DI Knox said, "We will continue this conversation at the station."

Montell wasn't listening. "I had a reading with her three months ago. I wanted her to get rid of my bad luck. She charged me three hundred pounds. I didn't mind. I thought my luck had changed after the reading. She phoned me two days after I'd seen her. She told me a house had come up for sale. A bargain of a house. I said I didn't want to move, but she convinced me to. Said it was fate and would lead to something amazing. It was all part of my increasing good luck, that's what she said. If I didn't buy the house, my bad luck would return with a vengeance."

"Mr Collins," DI Knox attempted to stop him.

He waved his arm around the room. "It was this house. I bought it from Jed Humphreys. He was keen to sell and offered me less than the market price on the basis of the sale going ahead quickly, and without solicitors and searches. I agreed. I thought I was getting the best end of the deal. But I was wrong. Four weeks after I'd moved in, I got a letter from the council saying they were going to knock down my house. They said something about collapsed mines nearby, and that the houses on this street weren't safe. They were responsible for the demolishing costs for some legal reason. I can't remember what that was now. They offered me half of what I'd paid to Jed. I spoke to some solicitors. They said I should take what the council offered and said the council were within their rights to knock my house down."

I asked, "Did you speak to Jed Humphreys about it?" I ignored the warning look which the inspector gave me.

"I couldn't find him," Montell admitted. "He gave me a number, but it was out of use. I didn't know what to do. I decided to speak to Theodosia again. I wanted to know if things were going to turn around for me. I thought buying the house was part of some big scheme which would end up with me getting rich. I didn't suspect Theodosia of lying to me. It took me weeks of phoning her before she finally agreed to see me again, and only at a public event. Looking back now, I think she was scared to see me on her own in her house. At the event, I recognised that young lass Verity, from photos in this house when it had belonged to Jed. I found out her last name when I went for my reading with Theodosia. She had a list of people on her table. It was upside down, but I got Verity's last name and her address. I was going to contact her so I could get Jed's whereabouts."

Peggy asked, "What did Theodosia tell you during your reading?" She also ignored the warning look which came her way from DI Knox.

Montell's voice was full of bitterness. "When she saw me at your café, she pretended she didn't recognise me. I soon reminded her who I was, and about the house she convinced me to buy. She said I had to be patient about the house. She said my reward would come, but I needed a spiritual cleansing before that could happen. Which I paid for. And I paid for those lottery tickets I told you about."

"Lottery tickets?" DI Knox said.

Peggy said, "Karis told you about those in your office. Don't you remember?"

DI Knox nodded. "Right. Yes." A look of resignation crossed her face. "Mr Collins, you may as well tell us the rest of the story."

"I'm trying to," he pointed out. "During the reading, I saw that notebook you're holding. Theodosia was scribbling in it just as I came around the curtain. I saw my name and a figure next to it. When it came to my cleansing and the lottery tickets, the amount of money I paid her matched up to the number she'd put in her book. She already knew how much she was going to charge me, even before I'd started talking. I knew then she was a scam artist. And I suspected Jed had scammed me too. When I left the café, I went online and found Verity which led me to her uncle. We met and had an interesting conversation."

"I bet you did," Peggy said. "What did he say? Did he know this house was going to be demolished when he sold it to you?"

"He'd heard some rumours. He asked around on the internet hoping someone would help him. He started to get ads from Theodosia offering to help with any housing issues people might have. He went to see her. She told him she'd find a buyer for his house if he paid her two thousand pounds." He jerked a thumb at himself. "I was the idiot who bought the house. There's something weird about Theodosia's ads because I started to see them too on some of the dating sites I went on. I was honest in my profiles and said I'd had nothing but bad luck all my life. That's how I found out about her because her ads kept popping up claiming to get rid of bad luck. I think I she targeted me on purpose."

"She did that to other people too," I said. "She must have been searching the internet for victims. Did you blackmail Jed into breaking into Theodosia's house and leaving his fingerprints behind?"

Montell's mouth twisted to the side as if deciding whether or not to continue.

"Answer the question," DI Knox ordered.

"All right. Yeah, I did. It was the least he could do after he tricked me into buying this useless house. I told him to steal that precious notebook of hers. I knew there was valuable information in it. I was going to blackmail her. I said he should break into other properties too over a couple of nights. It had to look genuine. I said if he didn't, then I'd tell his precious Verity he was a thief. Imagine how she'd feel if she knew that." He smirked. "I asked him if losing the respect of his niece was worth the two thousand pounds he'd paid Theodosia to find a buyer for this house. He agreed straight away. He knew the police would catch him. He was prepared to go to prison for a few years to protect his relationship with Verity. He was planning to tell her he'd been set up, but that there was nothing he could do about it."

I remembered the note I'd seen in my vision about Jed, and the amount of two thousand pounds written next to Theodosia's address. It wasn't an amount that someone was paying him. It was a figure he'd paid to Theodosia. Maybe he was carrying the note to motivate himself that evening.

"Why did you tell us Verity said she'd had a previous reading with Theodosia?" I asked.

His nasty smile sent shivers down my back. "I wanted to get her involved just in case Jed decided to tell some tales about me. Insurance, if you like." His smile vanished. "I never intended to kill Theodosia. I was just going to have a talk with her and get my money back."

"Liar," I said. "You hit her the moment she opened the door. She never stood a chance. Then you stole her notebook and the money she'd made from her other victims. You knew Jed was going to discover her dead body, and that he'd get the blame."

Montell attempted to look innocent, but it didn't last long. He started laughing. "I wish I could have seen his face when he saw her dead body. Serves him right for scamming me like that. I've been through hell these last months. As for Theodosia, she deserved it. Seeing the surprise in that woman's eyes when I hit her was so satisfying. Finding her money was a bonus. And the notebook too. I was going to plant it on Jed, but he went and got himself arrested too quickly. His luck is even worse than mine."

DI Knox looked at us. "We've heard enough. Leave this to me now. I'll be in touch."

Chapter 29

D I Knox put a finger under her nose. "What is that disgusting smell?"

I pointed to the sleeping twins. "It could be either one of those two. Or a combination of both of them." I turned in my seat. "It could be the kitchen. It's been chaos in there. Some toast was burnt earlier. A piece of fish was overcooked in the microwave. And a cake was left unattended in the oven. I have opened the windows, but it's going to take a while for the air to clear."

"How can you live like this?" she asked. She gingerly removed her finger.

"It's only for a few hours until my sister and brother-in-law wake up. They were desperate for sleep. As soon as they're awake, I'm going home. Take a seat."

"No, thanks. I'm not staying." She glanced at the babies. "Are they supposed to make that much noise when they're asleep? Why are they snoring so loudly? I thought babies were supposed to be quiet when they're asleep."

I said, "You should hear their parents, they're even louder. Are you sure you don't want a cup of tea? I've just put the kettle on."

"No. Thanks again. I just wanted to let you know about Theodosia's case."

"Oh? Did Seb ask you to?"

She shook her head. "No. I wanted to do it." She shuffled from one foot to the other. I'd never seen her look uncomfortable before. "I wanted to thank you for your help. Not that I believe in that psychic nonsense. Anyway, Montell Collins has been charged with her murder. He was happy to give us the full details. In fact, he wouldn't shut up about it. Seems to think it's all part of his bad luck and that it was going to happen one day."

"I can just imagine him saying that." I frowned. "There's something that's not making sense to me. I can't stop thinking about it."

There was almost a smile on the inspector's face as she said, "Let me guess. Is it about Jed Humphreys?"

"It is. I don't understand why he would break into Theodosia's house just to stop Verity finding out he's a thief. And to then go to prison for it."

DI Knox nodded. "That bothered me too. Until I spoke to Jed. He did those things because Montell threatened to hurt Verity. He showed Jed all the details he had about Verity. Where she lived, who her friends were, and where Verity worked. It was all the information he'd found online."

"He threatened to hurt her? Wow. That's horrible."

"I know. Montell Collins is a horrible man. He's got a nasty streak to him. He went into great detail about how Theodosia died. And how she deserved her comeuppance, as he called it." Her nose wrinkled. "Is that a new smell? It's disgusting."

"That'll be Charlie. He has a distinctive aroma. He's going to need a nappy change."

Her face filled with panic. "Now?"

"No. I'll wait until he wakes up. Are you sure you don't want to sit down?"

She edged towards the door. "No. I've nothing else to tell you. DCI Parker will be back next week. You probably already know that." She paused. "I'm not going to say anything about your previous cases with Seb. It's nothing to do with me. I'll see myself out. Thanks again for, you know."

I checked on the sleeping babies before walking her outside. A vision flashed into my mind as I followed her to the car. Like the fast-forwarding of a video, I saw DI Knox's professional life through the years. I saw how hard she worked, and how little recognition she got. I witnessed the long nights she worked in the office, and how she turned down invites because she wanted to study instead.

Out of nowhere, a voice came into my head. A female voice. I listened to her clear words. I pressed my lips together. Getting messages from departed ones was a new talent which I was not enjoying.

DI Knox unlocked her car and turned to me. "I apologise if I've been harsh with you."

"It's okay. I know how hard you work. You're not going to believe what I say next, but I can't do anything about that. I've just got a message from your mum."

DI Knox gave me an incredulous look.

I ignored it. "She said you work too hard and you need to get out more. Someone called Tim works with you. Your mum says he's been interested in you for years and has asked you out five times. He's going to ask you again. Say yes this time."

"Now, just a minute," she began to argue with me.

I held my hand up. "Your mum says it's time to move out of that pokey flat. You can afford something better. There's a cottage at the end of Primrose Lane which you'd love. You drive past it every day."

"You're making this up!"

"I'm not. I know the name your mum used to call you when you were little. Fiona Freckle-face."

DI Knox paled. "She did call me that. How do you...? I don't understand. She can't possibly have spoken to you."

"She did. That's all she said. Do what you want with that information." I smiled at her and added, "Fiona Freckle-face."

I said goodbye before returning to the house of disgusting smells. I silently sent a message to people in the afterlife and asked them to leave me alone.

But I had a feeling they wouldn't, and this was only the beginning.

About the author

I live in a county called Yorkshire, England with my family. This area is known for its paranormal activity and haunted dwellings. I love all things supernatural and think there is more to this life than can be seen with our eyes.

I HOPE YOU ENJOYED this story. If you did, I'd love it if you could post a small review. Reviews really help authors to sell more books. Thank you!

THIS STORY HAS BEEN checked for errors by myself and my team. If you spot anything we've missed, you can let us know by emailing us at: april@aprilfernsby.com

―――――∾――――

YOU CAN VISIT MY WEBSITE at: www.aprilfernsby.com[1]

―――――∾――――

FOLLOW ME ON Bookbub[2]
   Warm wishes
   April Fernsby

―――――――――――――――――

1. http://www.aprilfernsby.com

2. https://www.bookbub.com/authors/april-fernsby

Death Of A Psychic
A Psychic Café Mystery
(Book 8)
By
April Fernsby
www.aprilfernsby.com

Don't miss out!

Visit the website below and you can sign up to receive emails whenever April Fernsby publishes a new book. There's no charge and no obligation.

https://books2read.com/r/B-A-LQJE-TZYEB

BOOKS 2 READ

Connecting independent readers to independent writers.

Also by April Fernsby

A Brimstone Witch Mystery
As Dead As A Vampire
The Centaur's Last Breath
The Sleeping Goblin
The Silent Banshee
The Murdered Mermaid
The End Of The Yeti
Death Of A Rainbow Nymph
The Witch Is Dead
A Deal With The Grim Reaper
A Grotesque Murder
The Missing Unicorn
The Satyr's Secret

A Psychic Cafe Mystery
A Deadly Delivery
Tea and Murder
The Knitting Pattern Mystery
The Cross Stitch Puzzle
A Tragic Party
The Book Club Murder
Death Of A Psychic

Standalone
Murder Of A Werewolf
The Leprechaun's Last Trick
A Fatal Wedding
Psychic Cafe Mysteries Box Set 1
Brimstone Witch Mysteries - Box Set 1
Brimstone Witch Mysteries - Box Set 2
Brimstone Witch Mysteries - Box Set 3
Brimstone Witch Mysteries - Box Set 4
Brimstone Witch Mysteries - Books 1 to 13